Christmas is coming, the goose is getting fat, please put a penny in the old man's hat. Yes, but I first require more information about the goose, the penny and the hat. We can't be too careful these days. How fat is the goose getting and what connection does it have with the old man? Is the goose getting so fat that it is likely to explode with disastrous results for the nation? How will paying the old man prevent this outcome? The situation is unclear.

    I am on more certain ground when I explain that the following fictions have been assembled in their present form in order to celebrate the festive season. They include work from the span of the past quarter century. The first twenty-four tales form a sort of advent calendar from December 1st to 24th. Then it is Christmas Day and time for the stocking and the twenty-eight little tales inside it. Now all that remains is for me to bid you a Merry Xmas!

Yule Do Nicely

A WEIRD AND GHOSTLY ADVENT CALENDAR

(AND STOCKING TOO)

Rhys Hughes

Gloomy Seahorse Press

First Edition
Copyright © Rhys Hughes 2017

The right of Rhys Hughes to be identified as the Author of the work has been asserted by him in accordance with the Copyright, Design and Patents Act 1988.

All rights reserved. No part of this publication may be reproduced, stored in a retrieval system, or transmitted in any form or by any means without the prior written permission of the publisher and author, or be otherwise circulated in any form of binding or cover than that in which it is published and without a similar condition being imposed on the subsequent publisher.

All characters in this publication are fictitious and any resemblance to real persons, living or dead, is purely coincidental.

ISBN-13: 978-1976234835

ISBN-10: 1976234832

Gloomy Seahorse Press
http://gloomyseahorsepress.blogspot.com

Contents

The Hidden Sixpence 7
Three Friends 7
Down in the Park 10
The Chocolate Princess 12
Loafing Around 15
The Duvet Thief 18
My Beetroot Brow 22
The Moon and the Well 24
His Unstable Shape 25
The Cakes of Gehenna 29
Double Atlas 34
The Dirtiest Ararat 35
Zucchini Overdrive 40
Suttee and Sweep 43
The Strongest Monster 48
Cats' Eyes 50
Fringes and Bangs 51
Monsieur Choux 55
A Corking Tale 57
Don't Shoot the Messenger 58
All the Waiting 59
The Wrong Lamp 63
The Pancake Hurler 64
The Precious Mundanity 66

The Shocking Stocking 69
    Tarzan in India 69
    Nookie Nocking 71
    The Cockney Kharms 71
    The Log 73
    Wrexham Chainsaw Massacre 74
    The Opposite of Moons 75
    Fate and the Warrior 76

RASPBERRIES	76
THE RACE	77
THE MISCREANT	78
BLOCKING THE FLUE	79
THE HIDEOUS CACKLE	79
FOSSILISED HURRICANES	80
KHARMS BEFORE THE STORM	82
KEEP KHARMS AND BE AN ABSURDIST	82
KNOCK! KNOCK!	84
SUN SOUP	85
NOT A REAL POEM	85
IN MY OWN HANDS	85
THE FIGURE OF SPEECH	86
A POST-DISASTER STORY	86
PRETTY FACE	87
THE UNFAIR FUNFAIR	87
FORGETTING FACES	89
METAFICTION	90
GERONIMO	90
X MARKS THE SPOT	90
LIFE AFTER DEATH	91

THE ADVENT CALENDAR

THE HIDDEN SIXPENCE

A young man was visiting the family of his girlfriend over the Christmas period for the first time. "I don't believe in ghosts," he said, as she led him into the house. In the parlour they sat down together for dinner.

"Careful you don't swallow the hidden sixpence!" she warned, when the pudding was served.

"Cough, cough, cough, splutter!" he replied.

When he had recovered, she tenderly touched his arm. "What did I tell you? Puddings can be lethal at this time of year. You were lucky not to choke to death!"

He smiled in return but said nothing.

Concerned, she added, "Go into the kitchen and drink a glass of water. You'll find it through that door there."

Standing up and moving stiffly, he nodded and followed her advice, but he took a shortcut through the wall.

THREE FRIENDS

The three friends were mountain climbers who had trekked to the roof of the world. They had encountered many dangers on the way and each had taken a turn to plunge down a crevasse. Bound together by ropes as well as friendship, it seemed they had all escaped death by the narrowest of margins.

One by one, they had praised their luck and had agreed that teamwork was wonderful.

After the end of one particularly difficult day, as the crimson sun impaled itself on the needle peaks of the horizon, the three friends set up their tent on a narrow ledge. The first friend, who had survived the first crevasse, boiled tea on his portable stove and lit his pipe. Stretching out his legs as far as the ledge would allow, he blew a smoke ring and said:

"Do any of you know what day it is? It is the second day of December. While timid souls are snug indoors, we are out in the cold. The wind whistles past this mountain like the voice of a ghost, shrill as dead leaves. The icy rock feels like the hand of a very aged corpse. Those lonely clouds far away have taken the form of winged demons."

Then after a pause he added, "Everything reminds me of the region beyond the grave. I therefore suggest that we all tell ghost stories, to pass the time. I shall go first, if you like."

Huddling closer to the stove, the first friend peered at the other two with eyes like black sequins. "This happened to me a long time ago. I was climbing in Austria and had rented a small hunting lodge high in the mountains. Unfortunately, I managed to break my leg on my very first climb and had to rest in the lodge until a doctor could be summoned. Because of a freak snowstorm that same evening, it turned out that I was stuck for a whole week. The lodge had only one bed. My guide, a local climber, slept on the floor.

"Every night, as my fever grew worse, I would ask my guide to fetch me a drink of water from the well outside the lodge. He always seemed reluctant to do this, but would eventually return with a jug of red wine. I was far too delirious to wonder at this, and always drank the contents right down. At the end of the week, when my fever broke, I asked him why he gave me wine rather than water from the well. Shuddering, he replied that the 'wine' had come from the well. I afterwards learned that the original owner of the lodge had cut his wife's throat and had disposed of her body in the obvious way..."

The first friend shrugged and admitted that his was an inconclusive sort of ghost tale, but insisted that it was true nonetheless. He sucked on his pipe and poured three mugs of tea. Far below, the last avalanche of the day rumbled through the twilight. The second friend, who had survived the second crevasse, accepted a mug and nodded solemnly to himself. He seemed completely wrapped up in his own thoughts. Finally, he said:

"I too have a ghost story, and mine is true as well. It happened when I was a student in London. I lived in a house where another student had bled to death after cutting off his fingers in his heroic attempt to make his very first cucumber sandwich.

"I kept finding the fingers in the most unlikely places. They turned up in the fridge, in the bed, even in the pockets of my trousers. One evening, my girlfriend started giggling. We were sitting on the sofa listening to music and I asked her what was wrong. She replied that I ought to stop tickling her. Needless to say, my hands were on my lap.

"I consulted all sorts of people to help me with the problem. One kindly old priest came to exorcise the house. I set up mousetraps in the kitchen. But nothing seemed to work.

"The fingers kept appearing on the carpet, behind books on the bookshelf, in my soup. I grew more and more despondent and reluctantly considered moving.

Suddenly, in a dream, the solution came to me. It was a neat solution, and it worked. It was very simple, actually. I bought a cat..."

The second friend smiled and sipped his tea. Both he and the first friend gazed across at the third friend. The third friend seemed remote and abstracted. He stared out into the limitless dark. In the light from the stove, he appeared pale and unhealthy. He refused the mug that the first friend offered him.

The first two friends urged him to tell a tale, but he shook his head. "Come on," they said, "you must have at least one ghost story to tell. Everybody has at least one." With a deep, heavy sigh, the third friend finally confessed that he did. The first two friends rubbed their hands in delight. They insisted, however, that it had to be true.

"Oh, it's true all right," replied the third friend, "and it's easily told. But you might regret hearing it. Especially when you consider that we are stuck on this ledge together for the rest of the night."

When the first two friends laughed at this, he raised a hand for silence and began to speak. His words should have been as cold and ponderous as a glacier, but instead they were casual and tinged with a trace of irony. He said simply:

"I didn't survive the third crevasse."

DOWN IN THE PARK

There had been another report of a flying saucer over our town and this time I believed it. I saw it with my own eyes, not with anyone else's, when I rose in the early hours to fetch a glass of water back to my bedside table. Flashing lights, weird flight path, eerie low drone and no sign of any trickery at all.

It hovered above my garden briefly, as if waiting for something, but I didn't run out in my pyjamas; the grass was wet and I couldn't find my slippers. So I forsook the opportunity.

The next morning I met Clive in the bakery. I was buying iced buns and so was he, but to my mild surprise he also bought a pizza, vegetarian, with a topping of extra olives.

"Did you hear about the—" I began.

"Yes, Douglas, yes; I saw it myself and I stood and wondered. It hovered above many gardens, including mine, and then moved on. What purpose did it have? I pondered long and suddenly I realised!"

"You did what?" I croaked.

"I realised the truth about them, about the flying saucers. I know what they are and why they come here. I'm going to the park now and if you accompany me there I'll explain everything."

The chance was too good to miss, so I followed Clive along the street that led to the nearest park. When we got there we gravitated to the lake, as always, and watched the ducks. I munched on an iced bun and cast my spare crumbs into the ripples.

The ducks were happy to eat the morsels I offered them, but Clive held my arm in a powerful grip, most unlike him, and stopped me casting more pieces. "Watch this!" he cried.

Like a discus thrower he span on the spot and cast his pizza as far as he could. It was still warm and the olives glittered like crystals and steam rose from the tomato paste as it soared over the waters. I know little about the aerodynamic properties of Italian cuisine, but it seemed to hang in the air for ages. Then it dropped into the lake and sank.

"I was expecting it to float," I remarked feebly.

But Clive was ecstatic. "Did you see? The ducks misunderstood it! They simply didn't know what to *make* of it! They didn't recognise it as food and why should they? That proves my point!"

I frowned. "You mean that—"

"Yes, Douglas, yes! Flying saucers are scraps of food that are being thrown to us by aliens from outer space. It's so obvious! Why has no one thought of this before? We throw food for ducks; the aliens throw food for us. It's a perfect analogy!"

I didn't believe him and I told him so. But that same night I moved my dining table and a solitary chair into my garden and sat there, expectantly, with a knife and fork.

I'm still there, waiting. And I've drunk all the wine.

THE CHOCOLATE PRINCESS

Of all the countries in Africa, Côte d'Ivoire has the best beaches and it is also the country that produces most of the chocolate in the world. In fact it has so much chocolate growing on the trees that people can't eat all of it and they have to do other things with it.

One way of using up all the extra chocolate is to make houses and clothes from it. Bricks of hard chocolate are used to build the houses and layers of soft chocolate are used to make the clothes.

There was a young girl called Emmanuella who was walking along the beach one morning. The day was as lovely as a smile. As she passed a hut on the sand, an old woman poked her head out and called to her. This old woman had twinkling eyes.

"I have just made a beautiful dress out of some chocolate and I need someone to model it for me," she said.

Emmanuella asked, "You want me to be your model?"

"Yes," said the old woman.

Emmanuella was very surprised when she saw the chocolate dress. It was flavoured with mango, papaya, coconut and avocado. She tried it on and although it was a bit sticky it suited her. The old woman had a long mirror in her hut and Emmanuella twirled round and round and round so she could see herself from every angle.

"I look delicious in this dress," said Emmanuella.

"In that case you can have it," the old woman kindly said, "but don't wear it at midday when the sun is hottest, otherwise it will melt all over you and then you will have to swim in the sea to get clean, but swimming in the sea is a bad idea too."

"Thanks for the advice," replied Emmanuella.

She took the dress with her, and that same night in the city of Abidjan she went dancing in a club where all the records on the turntables were made from chocolate and the drinks that were served were chocolate but flavoured with palm wine. The music that was played came in two kinds, milk and plain, and the palm wine was ordinary red wine but poured into the palm of the hand. This makes sense.

"You look just like a princess!" said a young man who came up to ask Emmanuella to dance with him.

"Merci, I'm indeed a princess," she lied, because it was fun to pretend to be something that she wasn't.

They danced together and it was very nice, just a bit sticky, because the dance floor was made from chocolate. But they arranged to meet the following day and the young man said he would treat her to dinner. He promised to take her to the most expensive restaurant in the city, which was the only place in Côte d'Ivoire that served food that wasn't made from chocolate. Even the soup was real soup and not chocolate syrup, as it was in all the other restaurants.

Tomorrow came and Emmanuella was very excited and she put on the chocolate dress again, even though it was the second day running she had worn it, but that was fine because she changed her hair and had different bracelets. The bracelets were made from chocolate and her hair clips also. The name of the country should surely be changed to Côte de Cocoa, but such decisions aren't mine to make.

She met the man, who was called Alexandre, and they went into the restaurant and they had fried plantains, baked yams, breadfruit, calalou, pilau rice, red beans, groundnuts, attiéké, ugali, and all of it was real, and even the musicians who played for them used instruments that were real instruments and not chocolate guitars.

When the meal was over, Emmanuella said, "Merci, mon cherie, but I think it must be very expensive."

"Oui, but that doesn't matter because you are a princess."

"This is generous of you," she said.

Alexandre frowned. "No, it is generous of *you*. I am a poor man but you are a princess and that means you have lots of money."

"Oh no!" cried Emmanuella.

It was too late to run out of the restaurant because they were so full of food that they could only move slowly. So when the waiter came and they were unable to pay, he summoned the manager, who was angry and made them do all the washing up in the kitchen as a punishment.

Emmanuella never saw Alexandre again, and she stopped liking the dress too. For her it became a terrible thing like a headache, a reminder of the embarrassing situation in the restaurant. The following day she wore it out on the beach at midday and allowed it to melt all over her. This was a deliberate act, a form of sweet atonement.

Then she was very sticky and had to go for a swim.

But so many chocolate pods had fallen from the trees into the sea over many years that even the sea was now made from chocolate. Emmanuella finally understood the old woman's warning. When she emerged from the waves she found that she was wearing chocolate clothes again, but not an elegant dress, just a shapeless covering.

She sighed and continued her walk along the beach, one of the best in Africa, and that was the end of that.

LOAFING AROUND

They paddled the canoe up the creek to the rotting jetty. In the last rays of the setting sun, they climbed onto the creaking planks and made their way to dry land. The town was silent. No light shone in any window. The rain still dripped from the sagging balconies.

"Looks like we're too late," said Worthington.

Nashe shook his head. "We can't be certain of that yet. We'll have to check every single house one by one."

Worthington puffed out his cheeks. "This town has been cut off from civilisation for hundreds of years. Who knows what affect the toxins had on the people who lived here? I mean—"

"That's what we're here to find out. Come on."

But Worthington was wary. "The people of the last town had evolved into giants; and in the town before that, they only had one eye each; and in the town before that... Hideous!"

Nashe shrugged. "You knew the risks."

"Yes, I suppose I did. All the same, it's frightful."

"Let's get it over with, shall we?"

The beam of his heavy torch swinging ponderously in the twilight, his boots squelching dockside mud, he led the way along the waterfront to a row of buildings that turned out to be shops. It was weird seeing them in such a place, in a town surrounded by bubbling green swamps; they were too quaint, pleasant and picturesque.

"Bakers' shops!" breathed Worthington.

Nashe frowned. "All of them, without exception."

Worthington licked his dry lips.

"Look at this display. Braided bread! Seeded rolls and baguettes! And they are fresh. It's almost Christmas and one might expect festive loaves to be in the shops. This means that people still live here! The town isn't dead. But where is everyone? Are they hiding?"

Nashe pushed at the front door of every shop. They were all locked for the night with the exception of one at the end of the row. The hinges were oiled and the door swung smoothly open. The two men entered the shop. The torch beams played over shelves packed with bread and cakes. Then Worthington jerked his head and said:

"Shhh! I think I heard something, a rustling…"

Nashe froze, his ears prickling.

He nodded slowly, pointed at one of the largest loaves that stood on a low shelf. The noise was coming from inside it. Worthington joined him and rested his head against the crust.

He hissed, "There are voices within it!"

Nashe reddened, whether from rage or embarrassment was impossible to determine, and he used his free hand to claw apart the loaf. Fistfuls of fluffy bread were scattered in all directions. Worthington retreated a few steps in fear, but his companion was oblivious to danger. He tore with a primal savagery at the whispering loaf.

At last the truth was exposed. A cavern in the heart of the loaf, some sort of cunning refuge for mutants…

The people that were exposed were recognisably human, but none of them were taller than half an inch.

"They have degenerated over many generations!"

"The toxins did this! The toxins!"

"No, I think it was something even worse…"

Nashe was aghast and he rapidly retreated to where Worthington was standing. Both of them crowded the doorway of the shop. They took one last look at the miniature humans; then they ran out into the street, back to the jetty and the safety of the canoe.

"The worse outcome for any isolated community," growled Nashe as he paddled with all his strength to propel them back into the labyrinth of the bubbling swamp, home of snakes with arms and birds with plumage that flashed in colours that hadn't existed before the disaster. It took ten minutes of furious work before they felt secure enough to slow the pace and talk properly again to each other.

"Yes, the worst outcome," agreed Worthington.

"They were tiny! Like imps!"

"Smaller than that. Smaller than my thumb…"

Nashe shuddered and said in an undertone, "I've only ever seen such a situation once before. Down south."

"Horrible. Who could imagine that the entire population… I mean, the entire population… would be…"

"In bread," nodded Nashe with tragic eyes.

THE DUVET THIEF

An elaborate oak-panelled study with a leather couch. Dr Kennedy was a traditional therapist. The tools of his trade lay at strategic points about the room. Pendulums, tape recorders, the complete works of Jung. On a battered old record player, a disc etched with a hypnotic spiral revolved endlessly, a series of mirrors reflecting the resulting mandala to a screen positioned just above the patient's head.

The patient at this particular moment in time was a thin, nervous-looking man who had entered the study with stubble and a drooping cigarette obscuring his trembling chin. He had taken to the couch with as much enthusiasm as a pearl leaves its oyster. Dr Kennedy had frowned in a thoroughly professional way, pulled at his famous Swiss-style beard and clicked his tongue a dozen times, like a bat determining the range of a mosquito supper.

"Paul Artichoke?" Dr Kennedy looked at the list

his secretary had handed him earlier. He was used to his clients hiding their embarrassment under names so ill fitting that they were obviously pseudonyms, but this one was ridiculous enough to be genuine. "May I call you just Paul?"

"Call me anything you like."

Paul glanced suspiciously around the study. Portraits of the great psychiatrists hung all over the wall behind Dr Kennedy's chair. Someone had drawn a beard on the one of R.D. Laing, and stuffed a fat Havana cigar between his ascetic lips, both with a blue felt-tip pen, as if to bring this maverick back into the arms of orthodoxy.

"Wasn't he the one who said that schizophrenia was a sane reaction to an insane world?" Paul indicated the mutilated portrait. "He was quite popular when I was young."

"And quite wrong." Dr Kennedy smiled, but his eyes blazed with repressed fury. "It is not a reaction to any such thing. It is to do with the desire of the individual to assuage the guilt felt after indulging in various sexual fantasies directed at a mother/sister figure. But is this what you have come about? Schizophrenia?"

"No." Paul shook his head. "No, I have come about a more trivial problem. Trivial at the moment, that is. Actually, I have come about my wife."

"So your wife is insane? I thought as much. But I don't know what I can do for her. We might as well face facts. She will have to come in alone. The treatment might involve some physical activities. Release of sexual inhibitions, that sort of thing. Is she good looking?"

Paul waved Dr Kennedy to silence. "My wife is not mad. No, my problem is something else entirely. It concerns our sleeping arrangements."

"Of course. Sex is always the key. She is frigid, eh? Perhaps she is attracted to other women? They sometimes let you watch, you know."

Now it was Paul's turn to frown. "I don't think you understand. It has nothing to do with sex. Nothing at all. It's to do with the duvet we sleep under."

"Perhaps you should try mechanical aids. Vibrating apparatus and suchlike. And be sure to give me a full report. A few photographs as well…"

"I don't think you're listening, doctor. Our sex life is fine. I'm talking about the duvet we use to keep warm. We have a king-sized bed and the duvet in question is a large one. But in the middle of the night my wife keeps rolling over. The duvet ends up entirely on her side and I am left out in the cold."

"Have you tried lubricating fluids?"

Paul sighed and propped himself up on his elbows. "Do I have to spell it out for you? I'm not talking about sex. We have no problems with that side of our marriage. What I'm trying to get through to you is the fact that every night, in the early hours before dawn, I wake up shivering. I look across in the gloom and see my wife snuggled up tight in the duvet. But the duvet is meant for both of us. I've tried talking to her, but it's no use. Every night the same thing happens."

"Perhaps she should leave you for a more virile man…"

Paul was exasperated. He swung his legs over the side of the couch and stood up. "Well, I never expected this, you can be sure. I thought that you people were supposed to be sympathetic and helpful!"

Dr Kennedy grew anxious. He could see money slipping away through the gaps between his clubbed fingers. "Don't go! I was only joking. Part of the cure, you see. Don't worry. Have a cigar? I'm quite a respected figure, you know. I've met lots of rich people. Now what were you saying? Your wife is a nymphomaniac? Was that it?"

"No, no, no!" Paul screamed and waved his fists in the air. Dr Kennedy nodded, tugged at his beard again and took out a little notebook. He wrote the words *PSYCHOPATHIC TENDENCIES* on the crisp white paper and picked his nose.

"Listen," said Paul, with admirable restraint. "I have a wife whom I adore. Every night we make passionate love. We are both perfectly normal in that respect. Afterwards we fall asleep together. In the middle of the night I wake up and discover that the duvet is wrapped around my wife and that I am exposed to the chills of the night. She is oblivious of this fact. I am cold. I hate being cold."

"You are impotent then?"

Paul had been pushed beyond anger. His voice was very calm as he replied to Dr Kennedy. His breathing was as regular as that of the sea before a typhoon. "My one complaint in life is the fact that my wife always seems to steal the duvet. It is possible, however, that I might shortly add another grudge to the list."

"Ah yes, the duvet!" Dr Kennedy lowered his eyes. "Please forgive me. I have not been feeling well lately. Perhaps I need to talk to someone about my troubles? Please continue. Your wife keeps taking the duvet, you say? How does this make you feel?"

"Cold," replied Paul.

"Not resentful? Or bitter? Or twisted?" Dr Kennedy's eyes sparkled once more. "Do you not want to smother her in her sleep? Or slip a knife between her ribs?"

"Certainly not!" cried Paul. "It wouldn't be feasible anyway. For the last time, let me explain. My wife is a duvet thief. She steals the duvet in the middle of the night. When she steals the duvet I am left without any cover. I begin to shiver. I find it very difficult to fall asleep again. In the mornings I am always tired."

Dr Kennedy scratched his overlong forehead and studied Paul carefully through his little round glasses. He sighed deeply and shook his head. "Is that all? In that case, I think that you have been wasting my time. You tell me that talking to her is no use? Why don't you ask one of her friends to have a word with her?"

"She hasn't got any friends. Listen, doctor, it may sound like an absurd problem to you, but it's wearing me down physically and mentally. I desperately need your help!"

Dr Kennedy removed his glasses and rubbed his tired eyes. "I see. Well then, the only thing I can suggest is that you bring her to me and I'll try to reason with her."

"Oh no, I couldn't do that!"

"Why not?" Dr Kennedy yawned and blew his nose in a green handkerchief. "What reason could you have for not bringing her in?"

Paul grimaced and a tear trickled down his cheek.

"She's been dead for eight years."

MY BEETROOT BROW

I went to a ghost story festival last night. It was a bit disappointing. The ghosts took turns telling tales that were full of clichés. One ghost told a story about how he went hitchhiking and was picked up by a driver who didn't vanish and who turned out to be a living human being! Can you imagine anything so redundant? The only thing I can imagine more redundant than that is the accountant who is my neighbour and who was told by his boss last week that his services were no longer required. He dwells upstairs and I often hear him pacing the floorboards. This is an old building with rotten joists and my ceiling sags whenever he does that.

One day soon, although I don't yet know it, the ceiling will stop sagging and I will wonder why. Has he lost so much weight through worry than he no longer bends the floorboards? Has he gone out at last? But I didn't see or hear him vacate his room, where he has been holed up since he was ejected from the office where he worked, so I don't think that's the answer either. Then I will notice the shadow of a noose on the pavement. The morning sun has climbed high enough to slant through his windows at the precise angle needed to reveal his suicide to me. The beams are spearing through his apartment from one side to the other.

The weight of his dangling body on its rope, the rope connected to his ceiling by a hook, makes the floor of the room above him sag. The sag has been relocated up one level, in other words. When my own floor begins to sag and I am not pacing across it, I know that the man who lives below me has also hung himself. He is the boss of the accountant and he can't bear the awful guilt that comes with the suicide of his former employee. Luckily this is all in the future, so I can think about it without palpitations. My palpitations are quite unlike yours. First I will ponder the fate of the accountant, because it is nearer in time to the present.

I call the police and they come to cut him down and I know that if I ever attend a ghost story festival in the future, he will be there, his spirit recounting a tale about an unfortunate accountant who was misunderstood by the world. You know how it is. I do have sympathy for him, but his number was up, and when that happens you have no choice other than to accept it, especially if you are an accountant. I have my own problems anyway. I am a vegetable man, not a meat human, and this causes me many kinds of difficulty you never have to experience. Have you ever walked past a sauna and thought it was the soup of your doom?

I am getting old, just the same as you are, and there are wrinkles on my brow that are similar to yours. Similar but not the same. The wrinkles on my brow, my beetroot brow, are like the lines of a musical stave. There are no notes on it yet, so I can't say what my forehead sounds like, but I hope it will be something *jazzy* when it happens and not something *festive*. How I detest this season! The days are short and the nights are long and I am a vegetable man. I need those sunbeams to slant over me, to spear me right through. The notes will come. They will be spots of canker, the same way a pimple might be a note on your own brow stave.

THE MOON AND THE WELL

Once again, the moon is setting behind the old well at the bottom of the garden. Our slack faces crowd at the window, noses pressed to frosty glass, eyeing the falling moon. Lower and lower it sinks until it has completely vanished. Once a month we wait for this moment, we ache in the silence. At other times, rocking on our wormy chairs, rubbing our bony knees in front of a dying fire, we seek to fill space with songs and timid stories. But no words can emerge from our drooling mouths. We need the laughter of a child, the warmth of youth. We listen for the sound, the splash of water that will redeem us.

Together, trembling hand in hand, we race down the garden path, dragging our nets behind us. We have not been deceived. Our long wait is over. What a Christmas gift! The moon has missed the horizon and fallen into the well. We pull up the gurgling moon in a bucket and plunge our nets into the depths. The moon struggles beneath the silver liquid, a ladder of moonbeams rippling on the waves of emotion that sweep over us. It is a very new moon. From now on, the nights will always be dark. In the corner of a ruined cottage we will set up a cot. Through the bars of this cot we will feed our lunar child with a long-handled spoon.

His Unstable Shape

Most of us know that Humpty Dumpty was a large sentient egg who liked to sit on walls despite his unstable shape. He fell off and was broken and that is all that is certain about his life. Various apocryphal stories have become associated with him since his accident. Some people insist he was a philosopher as well as an egg. Others claim he invented a new emotion quite unlike any other emotion in the history of the world, but they are unable to describe what it might feel like. One professor has insisted that he was not an egg but the hull of an alien spacecraft from a distant star or a time machine from the future.

My aim today is not to add to this unhappy catalogue of fictions. I have no tales to tell about the kinds of antics he performed, nor can I offer insights into his character, beliefs or aspirations. Instead I wish to ponder something that is talked about too seldom. If Humpty Dumpty was an egg, what thing would have hatched out of him? Had his shell not been shattered by an external force, we may assume it would have been broken by an inner one, for the ovoid stage of his existence could only be brief and something within must have emerged to escort his identity further along the path of natural development.

No forensic evidence was collected in the wake of his death and our speculations remain purely notional. Yet I think it is possible to construct a plausible scenario using inductive logic alone. First we must attempt to establish what kind of egg he was, reptilian, amphibian or avian. One clue is his propensity for sitting on the tops of walls. It is true that lizards are accomplished wall climbers but they tend to cling to the sides rather than dominate the summits. Amphibians have no interest in walls that are not made of water and while they might congregate at waterfall tops they are disinclined to balance on narrow brick ledges.

There is always the possibility that he was the egg of some organism hitherto unknown on the surface of our world, that he might have come from outer space, from subterranean realms or an alternative dimension. But there is no need to multiply entities beyond necessity and without evidence to point us in that direction, it is safer to continue to assume that he was the egg of a phylum familiar to our zoologists.

Personally I favour the avian origin as the most realistic. Birds are constantly perching on our walls and sometimes they fall off too, when icy winds howl or rascals in the neighbourhood acquire new catapults.

Most of us are familiar with impetuosity and impatience. We might be reckless individuals ourselves or have friends and relations who embody the blurred spirits of haste and risk. Humpty was eager to become the bird he was destined to be, whatever kind it was, so keen in fact that he acted prematurely. Instead of remaining in the nest, wherever that was located, he left it and engaged in activities that were too old for him. He perched on walls, yes indeed, but perching high safely is the prerogative of those with wings. He was an egg and probably ignorant of the laws of physics. His fall was almost a foregone conclusion.

Now it is appropriate to turn our attention to the kind of bird he would have become if circumstances had been different. He was a large egg, one sizeable enough to hold audible conversations with human interlocutors*, so we may immediately dismiss the vast majority of our feathered friends as candidates. This leaves us with the ostrich, the rhea, the moa, and that extraordinary bird from the island of Madagascar, *Aepyornis maximus*, so enormous that it inspired the fable of the roc, the bird that swooped down to seize elephants in its talons. However, no sentient examples of these birds' eggs have been found.

All those birds are based in remote countries, and we are compelled to wonder how an individual egg might cross the oceans that separate these species' homelands from our own, for it was in England that

---

* See *Through the Looking Glass* for more details.

Humpty had his crisis and those birds are flightless. The ostrich and rhea are too small anyway, and the others went extinct before Humpty Dumpty existed. The more we consider the matter, the less likely it appears that he was the egg of a bird known to science. Thus we draw the conclusion that he was the egg of an undiscovered bird. What might the bird have been like? Because there are no clues there is no reliable answer to this.

But there is a solution that has an elegant absurdity about it and for that reason alone I am inclined to favour it. Some years ago I happened to be strolling through the city of Cologne. I stopped in order to check the time on my wristwatch, for I am one of those unfortunate fellows who are unable to read numbers and dials while on the move. As I lifted my wrist to my face, a loud creaking above my head made me fear that an object was about to fall on me. I looked up. It was a cuckoo clock fixed to the exterior wall of an old clock shop, one of the largest cuckoo clocks in the world. And it was striking the hour.

The hatch doors were opening, ponderously and painfully, and when they were fully agape the monstrous cuckoo came out. It emerged with a great deal of mechanical effort on an extendable trellis that sagged at its furthest reach. Then the cuckoo widened its beak and after an unsettling pause gave forth a cry of astonishingly dismal cadence. It repeated this sound three times to indicate that the local time was three o'clock in the afternoon and then, as exhausted as a senescent gran, it withdrew into its sanctuary, the hatch doors slamming behind it and the whirring of internal cogs ceasing as abruptly as they had begun.

I was astonished and affronted. I felt an outrage had been committed against my consciousness, that this clock was an insult to public decency, and I found myself wishing some other bird occupied the clock instead of an unmusical cuckoo. And it occurred to me that a different bird *had* once done so. Certainly it must. We all know the cuckoo's life cycle. It hatches in a nest not its own and destroys the other eggs in order to be the solitary recipient of all the attention from the bereaved parents. If cuckoos occupy clocks then it logically follows that some other bird once lived in them. But probably not a phoenix.

What bird lived in the clock before the cuckoo? This question is the key to understanding Humpty Dumpty's true identity. That is what I now believe, at any rate. Somewhere in this peculiar world of ours the decayed remains of a cuckoo clock may be found, a cuckoo clock vaster by many orders of magnitude than the one I saw in Cologne. The bird that was its original occupant was the one who laid Humpty Dumpty and eggs similar to him. A cuckoo invaded the nest and left an egg that hatched first and rolled out the others. Humpty Dumpty did not break on that occasion. The start of his life was a rehearsal for his death.

The Cakes of Gehenna

When Satan fell out of a high tree and broke his back, the workings of Hell were thrown into turmoil. Not that this was a disadvantage; the fiery pit thrived on chaos and confusion. But the lesser devils and demons grew insecure in their positions, they quarrelled and began to neglect their duties. A depression settled over them all.

Into their cloven clogs stepped their wives. They convened on the banks of the Acheron to discuss what needed to be done. The mystery still remained as to what Satan had been doing up the tree in the first place. Scrumping apples, Mrs Moloch said. That was the Serpent's job, Mrs Beelzebub reminded everyone. So where had the Serpent been at the time? Shirking responsibilities, they concluded.

There was a precedent for this peculiar state of affairs. The previous month, God Himself had crashed his bicycle. His injuries had ended His mighty reign over the cosmos. It is difficult to be omnipotent with a fractured skull. He still rested in a bed surrounded by screens, for no one may look upon the divine countenance and live. Sometimes, at night, He took a short walk in the hospital grounds. More often, He visited the recreation room alone and played pool by Himself.

The angels had been devastated by this sudden loss. Unlike the devils, they had no wives they could turn to in their hour of need. They were all bachelors. Gabriel had once had a girlfriend but she had long since returned to Harrow, where his influence was minimal. Comic scenes, tinged with tragedy, followed as the angels desperately attempted to declare Heaven a republic, form a Senate and compile a Bill of Rights. They had finally settled on a Free-Market economy and now contented themselves with stuffing quilts for export.

There were rumours that Satan was going to be taken to the same Hospital as the one that held God. Some wagging tongues would even have it that they were going to be placed on the same Ward together. This never would have happened in the old days, but times were changing. Belts were being tightened, finances were being given precedence over patient welfare. There was little that could be done. Or so avowed the more knowledgeable of the gossip-mongers.

Mrs Belial and Mrs Baal decided that this was a superb opportunity to review the fundamental mechanics of the infernal regions. They were both liberal progressives. They subscribed to *Sight And Scream*, *New Eschatologist* and *Helle*. Some of the more traditionalist wives, such as Mrs Ashtaroth and Mrs Mammon, disapproved of their methods, but they did not try to hinder them. Although they favoured different techniques, they all shared a common goal: Plutonian reformation.

"For too long, the male devils and demons have had it their own way," said Mrs Belial at one meeting, her words amplified by the hollow ram's horn she used as a megaphone. "Now, at last, we have the chance to change things for the better, to make Hell a far more productive and efficient sort of place, to give better value for money than ever before. There is one thing that we must remember: the tortured souls down here with us are not sinners. They are customers!"

There was a flurry of assorted clapping and a few nods of approval. Mrs Belial gestured at the black flames that danced all around and at the legions of screaming spirits that writhed in their midst. "Look at all this waste! Disorganisation is rife, as you would expect in any monolithic bureaucracy. There is no public accountability. We need quality control at every stage of the damnation process. Else how can we guarantee a satisfactory eternity of suffering and remorse?"

She then proceeded to announce ninety-seven major faults with the running of Hell and her solution to each of them. There would need to be a debate on these; the other wives would have to have their say. But the course of action she outlined seemed a sensible one. Unlike their husbands, who would have dithered for millennia, they resolved to begin implementing some of the more obvious changes immediately.

The first thing to do was to harness the energy that was not being used to torture sinners. Much of the heat of the fiery pit went straight through the walls and roof of Hell. This heat, as Mrs Moloch rightly suggested, could be used to run an almost infinite series of ovens. A cake business could be a useful sideline, as well as an outlet selling toasted muffins and bagels to passing tourists. (Mrs Baal had already made arrangements for the opening of the gates of Hell to sightseers from the upper worlds).

Indeed, as Mrs Asmodeus added, a system of turbines could also be constructed which could convert the rising hot air and sulphurous clouds into electricity. From this electricity, sewing machines and lathes could be powered. They would be able to sell hats and carved wooden idols as well as cakes. Or else the thrashings of the damned themselves could be somehow used to drive the whisks that would beat the eggs and flour. The possibilities were endless.

All this was inevitable, Mrs Beelzebub claimed, and could easily be confirmed by reading the final chapter of the Book of Fate (though she admitted that the last page of this book had been torn out by a prankster.) It would not take very long before the wives turned Hell into a successful concern, a boiling lake where anyone could hire out a paddleboat for an hour or two. Mrs Demogorgon's idea of setting up a suggestion-box for the benefit of screaming souls and visitors alike was little short of inspirational.

Hell would finally become what the consumer wanted it to be. One consequence of this, naturally enough, was that Heaven soon became depopulated. No-one wanted to sit around on fluffy clouds all day when they could just as easily spend an eternity of activity down below. The angels soon found themselves redundant and took to cribbage, pies and drugs. For some reason, they started wearing flat caps and braces. Theologians are currently studying this phenomenon.

Eventually, both Satan and God recovered from their accidents. But God had no desire to return to such a depressing providence, and Satan had been barred from Hell. They had become firm friends during their convalescence, patching up their differences and recapturing some of the mutual affection that had existed when Satan had been named Lucifer. They wonder if this reconciliation will herald a new age on peace on Earth.

Somehow they doubt it. They spend most of their time drinking in pubs in East Grinstead. It is not known why of all places in the universe this one was chosen for their sombre revels. As God explains, some mystery must still remain in our peeled and pickled cosmos. God wears a wide-brimmed hat and dark glasses; Satan prefers a coat whose collars protrude high above his head. Hunched in the shadows, they mull over old times. God carries a lightning-bolt in his pocket and Satan keeps a burning trident close at hand. Occasionally, when there is a jazz night in one of the bars, they try to join in. There is trouble then and the pair are usually ejected. But, man, they can sure singe the Blues.

Double Atlas

In the days of the Ancient Greeks, the titan known as Atlas was required to hold up the sky, and he used his shoulders to do this, his immense and appalling shoulders. His head bent forward and turned at an angle, his left cheek pressing against the underside of the sky, he kept absolutely rigid, for fear of shaking loose those things that were fixed deep in the heavens, the sun, moon and stars, and diverting the paths of those things that are a little lower, the lightning and clouds.

That was the Classical Atlas for you, the living pillar that stopped the sky from collapsing onto the world, but even if he had shrugged off his task, it might not have been the end of life down below. The sky would have landed on mountains and been pinned to their peaks, sagging from one summit to another, like an enormous deflating tent, and only on the plains of the Earth would it touch the ground and crush the inhabitants flat. The human race might continue.

Centuries later, Atlas' role was transformed. He no longer held up the sky but the planet itself, the entire globe, once again on his shoulders. I can't say which role he preferred. The sphere might be more awkward to balance, and a twitch or spasm in his muscles would agitate the oceans and cause them to lap his back with cold brine. If Atlas shrugged off his burden now and left the planet to its own devices, what would change? Nothing at all. Gravity would take over.

The planet wouldn't fall anywhere but continue its orbit of the sun. I suspect that Atlas was given an unnecessary task in both cases, as if the Gods who condemned him to such labour didn't know what use to put him to. They invented a pointless job for him.

Poor Atlas! I went to visit him, because I felt sorry for him, and flew there in one of our most reliable angels, peering out of the portholes along the body of the divine being as I crossed the intergalactic void.

As I entered your solar system and approached your planet, I was met with a most unexpected sight. We don't have things like this in our own galaxy. Atlas was still standing there with the Earth on his shoulders, but the Gods had forgotten to cancel the earlier Atlas, so there were now two of them, a pair of Atlases, and the one who held up the sky was standing on the globe that was balanced on the other one. The result of an absurd clerical error. The universe really is a bureaucratic mess.

THE DIRTIEST ARARAT

It was the grandest ship in the world. The captain stood on the deck and allowed the freezing wind to comb his white beard into a fork. He felt a mixture of pride and anxiety as the salt spray lashed his chest. Was the huge vessel really unsinkable? Her designer had been supremely confident at the launch, shaking his blueprints under the clouds and daring demons of the deep to drag her down. They were making good speed now, splashing into the dusk with lamps blazing, a wedge of carefree life and childlike trust on the bosom of a cruel sea.

The captain did not share the nonchalance of his crew. He was still unhappy about ignoring ice warnings received earlier in the day. Left to himself, he would have slowed the colossus, kept an eye out for floating obstructions. But his employer had goaded him into crossing the ocean as quickly as possible and it was better not to squabble with such powerful figures. Besides, this was no ordinary jaunt, but one which embodied the notion of human progress. The craft was a metaphor for the usurpation of brute nature by modern technology.

With a shiver, he turned and strode the polished boards back to the wheelhouse. The ship was constructed in three decks, each a labyrinth of watertight compartments, crowded with passengers of varying elegance. On the top level, the most cultured of his charges preened and chattered in luxury, nibbling at dainties. Below their feet lurked the middle orders, vainly aspiring to the fashions of their superiors. Right at the bottom, squirming in their own rage and filth, the third class occupants doubled as ballast. He cared for them all.

There was no quiet to be had anywhere. It sounded as if instruments were playing waltzes in every cabin. Soon it would be time for dinner, a ritual the captain despised. Sitting at a table laden with antique wines and complex meals, attempting to communicate with pretentious fools, was a duty which filled him with alarm. But he was stoical enough to bear it without raising his voice at any of them, however absurd their antics. A man who preferred to keep his opinions to himself, the captain tolerated the fuss as if it was bad weather.

This was his last voyage before retirement. When they reached port, he would throw his oilskins into the dock. He was idly dreaming of a dry future when a cry came from ahead:

"Iceberg! It's going to hit!"

"Hard to starboard!" he roared. But it was too late. With a violent lurch, the ship struck something large. Then the hull screamed as rivets popped and panels burst. He rushed out on deck. The fire of the floating mountain branded his eyelids. It was alive with a trillion trapped stars and each smooth facet cast them off as casually as a steward might flick spilt wine from a napkin. Ice is tough, he knew this. But the many edges of the mass were sharper than they ought to be. A goat's throat: that is what he felt his craft had become.

"There aren't enough lifeboats!" someone wailed.

"Aye, we're a sacrifice," he sighed. "Can't imagine why. Summon the designer. I want a word with him."

The panic was already surging down among the lower levels. He would have to use physical force to control the passengers before the mob mind overwhelmed sense and pride. He returned to the wheelhouse to search for something to serve as a club. The screams from the hold came to him like a pocket hell's echoes. He was still rummaging when the designer entered without knocking. "You called me?"

"I did. You claimed this ship was unsinkable."

The designer shrugged. "I guess there has been a change of plan. It isn't my fault. I simply obey the boss. I don't presume to know what his ultimate intentions are. Maybe he's decided to downsize this project for logistical reasons? He has his limitations too. He's only able to do his best with any specific situation."

"I don't understand. An insurance scam?"

"Unlikely. Let's step outside and take a closer look." The designer led the way back to the deck. Stopping at a rail, he indicated the burst of gorgeous stars on the bobbing mountain. "Now do you see? What type of glitter is this? The refractive index is quite different from that of an immense chunk of frozen water. From its general exterior, it absorbs and reflects very little light, but from a few places where the surfaces are favourable, there's lots of reflection and refraction, a brilliant array of flashings and translucencies. A skeleton of light. So I ask you: what substances behave in that manner?"

The captain removed his hat. "Diamonds."

"Precisely. Jetsam jewellery. But why would an enormous gemstone be floating on its own in the ocean?"

"A domestic crisis? A serious argument?"

The designer nodded. "His wife has decided to leave him. So she has hurled away her wedding ring. A symbolic action. We've collided with it. Alpha and Omega are now divorced."

"What am I supposed to do? Abandon ship?"

"Of course. But you'll be able to save less than one quarter of the passengers. He probably trusts you to make the right selection. He can't provide for them all now. Together, they planned to make a second world, but by himself he lacks the power. Well, life is unfair. I mean, look at me! I do his dirtiest work and I get constantly blamed for whatever goes rotten. But I just follow orders."

The captain quickly considered his options. He would rescue as many from the highest deck as possible, a few dozen from the middle, but only a couple from the bottom. There was no time for sentiment. The lifeboats had to be launched immediately. Every mammal and reptile should be safe. There was room also for the amphibians and birds. The bugs needed only a single boat, and he could easily spare that. The fish might take care of themselves, if they were slipped overboard. The worms could burrow under his armpits. He suddenly bellowed:

"Leave the mythological animals behind!"

Between the decks, there were security gates which were fitted with locks. When he heard the sliding of the bolts, he groaned and nearly had a stream of consciousness episode.

As the unicorns and centaurs rattled the bars, demanding justice or mercy, slurring their words like drunken fools, not that uncouth accents such as those were comprehensible even when they were sober, which never they were, pausing at frequent intervals to knock hooves and croon songs of pessimistic abandon, and dance the jig, hats perched on their unkempt heads at jaunty angles, the poetic rogues, to be sure, to be sure, make mine a pint of plain, for a pint of plain is your only man, he leapt into the last boat and hailed the designer.

"Don't you plan to come too?"

The designer shook his head. He clearly had his own way of leaving. He stumbled to the bow of the ship and climbed the rails with eyes shut. Then he opened them abruptly. His auburn horns did not blow in the wind. For an instant, he stood with arms extended, gazing across the grey sea. A pointless action, not justified.

"Look at me! I'm flying, Noah! I'm flying!"

Then he really was, spreading his leathery wings, flapping off into the stormy sky, forked tail lashing his buttocks as he ascended. Jealous of his freedom, the captain scorned the glamour of the incident. True, a rainbow appeared high above, but because it was the first there had ever been, he did not think to look up and notice. Besides, a similar optical effect might be produced by a mundane blow on the head. Certainly he was still concussed from the impact. And although romance was a contemporary style, because the time was ancient, this fact scarcely made it any more acceptable. Truth is truth. In the final analysis, the adventure, unlike the waters, had been very shallow.

ZUCCHINI OVERDRIVE

This event happened long ago in the mountains near Cercedilla, but not *very* long ago, just long enough, and the main protagonist was Don Cosquillas, who yearned to be a romantic hero, but wasn't. To be more specific he wanted to rescue a princess from a dragon and win her hand in marriage, and be granted half the lands owned by her father, presumably the king, as a bonus. Typical old-fashioned stuff. His wish wasn't granted in quite the way he expected but he did ride forth against a real dragon, something to be proud of, on a bicycle rather than a horse, a rusty machine now on display in the Venta de Leña. Go there and check!

Most people who talked of such things at all believed that dragons had died out in the Middle Ages. The date of this extinction was usually reckoned at about 1285 or so. Don Cosquillas always lamented the fact he had been born six hundred years too late, though the years themselves were never heard to agree on this point, and he bitterly cursed those knights who hadn't left any fire breathing monsters for *him* to tackle. One day a rumour reached his ears that high in the snowy peaks above Cercedilla a dragon had been sighted and so he lost no time cycling from Madrid to the village in question, the tails of his frock coat hissing behind like a forked tongue.

To his amazement nobody in Cercedilla seemed much concerned about the fabulous creature. They were only interested in the amazing new inventions of the era, such as telephones, sliced bread, ether, compression refrigerators and submarines, and regarded dragons as an unwelcome reminder of the superstitious past. They answered his urgent questions somewhat impatiently. "Yes, the beast is dangerous, and yes, it has taken a beautiful hostage, and yes, you have no rivals!"

As the only contestant in the game, Don Cosquillas relaxed a little. To fight a dragon at his own pace would be hard enough, but to race against other heroes intent on the same quest was asking too much. He had tender feet from his journey, sore buttocks too, and he decided to recover for a day before making the crucial assault. He probably armed himself, the details of this aren't clear, and when he was ready he slowly pedalled up the forest path towards the dragon's lair. All his assumptions about what he might encounter remained unchanged in his mind as he made the exhausting ascent. On the steepest slopes he dismounted and pushed his squeaking steed.

The following morning he returned, half victorious, half crestfallen...

"The dragon is a vegetarian!" he grumbled, as he displayed the object so easily rescued from the less than rapacious reptile, "and his hostage: a courgette!"

"We said it was beautiful," replied the inhabitants of Cercedilla, "and so it is."

"True," conceded Don Cosquillas, "but..."

"Return it to its rightful farmer and he may give you a reward," was the subsequent advice.

That's exactly what he did, and while the farmer who had grown the courgette was clearly overjoyed to be reunited with his beloved vegetable, he expressed this joy neither in word nor deed. Indeed his gratitude only manifested itself after repeated prompting by the hero, who kept crying, "I demand half your lands! That's the correct procedure. Or I'll hire a lawyer."

The farmer replied, "I'm rather poor and only own one field. You can have 50% of that, but if you're so keen on protocol you'll have to marry the courgette as well."

"Don't be absurd. I don't intend to settle down at my age!"

"You refuse the hand of my courgette? After spending the night alone with it up in the mountains. Kindly remain here while I fetch my scythe, you heartless molester..."

"Wait! Wait! I agree to your terms!"

"Good. I'll go and fetch the priest right now. No chance of a dowry, I'm afraid, not even a telephone, loaf of sliced bread or bottle of ether. And only the richest farmers around here can afford such luxuries as compression refrigerators and submarines..."

"Anything you say! I'll take the courgette as my bride!"

Thus the bachelor days of Don Cosquillas came to an end and he accepted his new role of husband with a long face, not a *very* long face, but long enough: he occasionally impaled soft biscuits on his chin. Eight or nine at a time. And he took the courgette back to Madrid and consummated the marriage, nobody knows how, not even he, and lived a life suited to the idiom of the city in that century, until things started to go wrong. And the years slowly passed, making those wrong things worse. Typical modern stuff. Then one day there was a knock at the door and his father in law stood on the threshold, coming to visit in the way relatives must do.

He gazed at Don Cosquillas and his unshaven chin, the dirty dressing gown and slippers, the half empty bottle of wine in one hand, the badly rolled cigarette burning close to a chapped lower lip, and he raised his rural eyebrows in disapproval and extended his brawny arms to catch the suddenly limp body of his son in law, who burst into tears and wailed:

"My wife has gone off!"

"Mistreatment at your hands, was it? Men like you sicken me. Where's my scythe? Damn, I left it in Cercedilla. Had an aubergine on the side, did you? Pulpo!"

And he stormed off in disgust, that farmer, and didn't return. As for Don Cosquillas, he never remarried. Bleak bitterness suited him, to a very minor extent, and drooling idiocy became an acceptable substitute for heroic romanticism. But he wasn't always lonely. The vegetarian dragon came to stay from time to time, overlapping orange scales clashing with the purple curtains, vast malodorous eyes like forgotten blue cheeses, tongue like unwashed frock coat tails, breath like patchouli joss stick fumes, to mount his bicycle and pedal furiously around his house in the highest possible gear. Because a story about a dragon that doesn't contain a description of that dragon is ridiculous.

SUTTEE AND SWEEP

"I need more space," said Mr Sweep to his wife.

Martha gritted her teeth. At first she had tolerated his growing introspection, his reversion to a childlike state, because she believed it was only a temporary reaction to stress. But six months had passed and he still showed no sign of emerging back into the adult world. On the contrary, he now wanted *more* time alone, not that he considered himself to be isolated in the basement he had converted into a private playroom. They had argued about that many times.

"Your puppets aren't real!" she kept insisting.

A crafty look would come into his eyes. "Of course they're real. What you mean is that they aren't alive, but you're wrong about that too. They *are* alive, all of them, Noddy is my favourite, he's my best friend and he listens to me."

"No he doesn't." She always felt too exhausted to reason with him.

"Noddy shows more understanding than you ever did. The other puppets are fine too, but Noddy's special. Some of the modern puppets are made of plastic but Noddy is wooden and his eyes are real glass. The others say stupid things in low whispers but Noddy only delivers nuggets of wisdom or remains silent. He never stops listening to me, though. He hears everything."

And so it went. She would throw up her hands in defeat and leave him to his own devices. Before moving to this house he had been relatively normal. Something about this place had changed him, started his obsession with puppets, compelled him to visit junk shops and jumble sales in an attempt to add to his collection. Now he had all the puppets he wanted and never went out.

Nor did he allow her to go down into the basement. Once, when he was fast asleep, she tiptoed down the stairs and switched on the light. The puppets stood in a large cardboard box in the centre of the room and she formed the distinct impression they were *disappointed* by her sudden arrival. A curious illusion.

"I need more space," Mr Sweep repeated. "You're getting in the way."

"You need a psychiatrist," responded Martha.

"No, I'm not mad, you don't understand. I know that puppets aren't normally alive, but mine are different, at least they are different *here*. My puppets can dance if they want to, and in fact they are constantly dancing in their souls, but they don't physically move for my sake. They told me why. Puppets build up a lot of resentment over the years, forced to move and jump at the whim of a human owner, with no choice in the matter."

"Puppets don't have souls, you fool!"

"Martha, listen to me. All that resentment eventually becomes a blind force. Provided the status quo isn't disturbed, everything will be fine, but if they are ever compelled or urged to move *on their own* all that pent up energy will be unleashed at once. That's when they will become truly dangerous. Imagine an avalanche of puppets! But it's fine right now, just dandy. They dance deep down inside only. This is a holy place for them. Our home, I mean."

She snorted in derision. "Why?"

"Because it has been built on the site of a puppets' graveyard!"

She wanted to beat her fists against the top of his head, but she restrained herself and plotted a more subtle revenge. She decided to use his delusions against him. The following morning she went out for an hour, killing time in the park but returning with a great show of excitement, slamming doors and calling for him. He emerged reluctantly from the basement, his eyes full of annoyance but not suspicion.

"Something strange just happened!" she gasped.

"What was it?" he muttered.

"I went shopping and took a short cut through the park and I came across a group of puppets balancing in a tree. It was almost as if they were lost and trying to get their bearings by studying the landscape from a higher vantage. I could swear they were alive! I ran back as fast as possible to tell you."

"What did they look like?" Mr Sweep bellowed.

"One of them was a very old gnome, another was a policeman, a third was a clockwork mouse, and I also noticed a wobbly man, a set of anthropomorphic skittles, a pair of goblins and a sort of bunny-monkey hybrid."

Mr Sweep's eyes bulged. "Are you serious? Those are all Noddy's friends! His friends from the original Noddy books! They must be searching for him! I'd better go and find them."

"I'm sure they're still there," said Martha.

He hurried out and Martha grinned to herself. Then she set to work building a fire in the unused grate in the front room. For the first time in many months she felt alive, suffused with joy, vengeful, energised.

As for Mr Sweep, he scoured the park in vain, squinting up at each tree and shuddering with an unspecified fear. He had a touch of agoraphobia due to his long confinement indoors but he forced himself to continue until the light began to fade. He was bitterly disappointed and returned home slowly, imagining that the lost puppets had climbed down from the tree and gone off in the wrong direction. What was wrong with them? Couldn't they detect the emanations of the puppets' graveyard and use that to guide them?

But he cheered up when he reached his front door and saw the note taped there. He read the first two lines of it and was so delighted he snatched it into his hand, entered his house, slid the bolt and piled the hallway furniture against the door. He was scared Martha might change her mind and come back.

The beginning of her note said: "I have gone forever. You wanted more space and so I now give you all the space you could ever need..."

He danced into the front room. Alone with his puppets at last! He was laughing so hard, his eyes were so blurry with tears of happiness, that it was a full minute before he understood there was a fire in the hearth. He blinked and his blood turned to acid. Then he was up and running to the kitchen for a pan of water. It took several trips to extinguish the abominable blaze.

Martha had ignited the entire box of puppets!

The individual figures weren't utterly consumed yet. Some of the plastic models had melted over the others and hardened under the impact of the cold water. Mr Sweep found himself gazing at a monster composed of many charred and twisted limbs and mutant heads, the vilest abortion in the history of puppetry. And it moved! The level of resentment was simply too high to repress any longer. The disgusting mess in the grate was alive and it wanted revenge on the nearest human!

Only Noddy had been spared, his favourite puppet, because Mr Sweep had taken him to the park. Noddy fell out of the wide pocket of his jacket and lay on the floor, idiotic head bouncing on its spring.

The rest of Martha's note said: "You are married to those damn puppets but you are dead to me. Do you know what happened long ago in India when a man died? His wife was burned alive on his funeral pyre. Our marriage is dead and so I have incinerated those who you loved. There is no puppets' graveyard here, only a crematorium!"

Mr Sweep was too terrified to move, but even if he had run it wouldn't have done him any good. His exit was barred.

Noddy kept nodding at his feet, still loyal but helpless.

Mr Sweep groaned. Why had he asked for more space? Space was terrible, a place where nobody was there to offer help.

The malevolent mass reached him. His mouth opened and something came out. A sound.

In space, Noddy can hear you scream.

The Strongest Monster

"How strong are you?" I asked the monster.

"I can lift the heaviest thing in the world!" was the answer.

"Can you lift infinity?"

The monster blinked maybe fifty eyes. "Of course not."

"But you can lift the heaviest thing in the world?"

"That's what I said."

"Are you willing to bet on it?" I suggested.

The monster scratched eighty ears with an equal number of fingernails. "Why not? But first we have to agree on the stakes."

"What are your usual terms?" I wondered.

The monster chewed two hundred lower lips in thought. "If I win, then I get to eat your entire extended family, all your friends and neighbours, everybody you have ever loved, and for dessert: yourself."

"That sounds reasonable," I said, "and I'll throw my work colleagues in for free."

"Very good. But what if *you* win?"

"There's no danger of that happening, is there? I mean, you are the strongest monster that ever was. How can you possibly lose?"

"Agreed. In that case, allow me to look for the heaviest thing in the world. I'll bring it back and lay it before you as proof."

I held up my hand. "No need to go anywhere."

"What do you mean?" cried the monster.

"Well the heaviest thing in the world is the world itself, isn't it? And that's directly beneath us. You've already found it!"

The monster nodded six hundred heads. "Then I shall lift the world."

I heaved a deep sigh. "I think you might be overlooking a crucial detail. To lift the world you have to lift everything on it, including yourself."

"I can do that," asserted the monster.

"But what will your lifted self be doing at the time? Lifting the world, that's what! So you will be lifting *his* world as well as your own."

"I don't follow you," said the monster.

"You'll have to lift this world, plus another world, the world you are already lifting. So you'll have to lift the world twice. And on that other lifted world you are also standing while lifting the world, which makes another world to lift, and so on forever!"

"Stop it! You are giving me a thousand brainaches!"

I shrugged. "You've already confessed that you can't lift infinity. So I guess I win the bet. Don't you admit defeat?"

"Very well, you are the victor," grumbled the monster.

"What about my prize?" I asked.

"You never specified what your stakes were," the monster pointed out.

"That's true. Allow me to state them now. I want you to eat my entire extended family, all my friends and neighbours, everybody I have ever loved — plus my work colleagues — and for dessert: yourself."

The monster snorted through one million nostrils. "You are a worse monster than I am!"

"That's right," I conceded. "You are just the strongest."

Cats' Eyes

We were on the right road. The presence of cats' eyes told us that nothing had gone amiss, that no errors of navigation had been made. In the darkness of a remote rural region during a moonless night it was a comfort to know that this line of glass studs would reflect our headlights and be a most reliable guide to our ultimate destination.

But something went wrong anyway. It was hard to explain why this should be so and I suspect I would decline the opportunity to know the reasons even if they were available. We must have taken an unintentional turning somewhere along our route. I said, "The cats' eyes have gone," and she nodded in the gloom and answered, "Dogs' ears."

It was true. This new road clearly had different rules to the old. The reflective glass studs had been replaced by flexible triangles that echoed every sound our vehicle made, including the conversations we held inside it, and threw the audio signals back at us, horribly amplified. "Turn off at the next junction," I advised and she did so.

But this new road was even stranger and more disturbing and certainly of less practical use. Lips puckered at us and we tasted afresh the meals we had lately eaten. "Weasels' mouths," she said, her frown so deep that it changed the outline of her face in profile when I glanced at her. We found another road and became more than hopelessly lost.

My nostrils were flooded with the bittersweet aromas of nostalgia, the pangs like vanilla, the regrets a new kind of smelling salts. "Aardvarks' noses! Who builds these roads?" I muttered. Every muscle in my body was tense. She maintained a steady speed but we both knew that morning would never appear in time. We took another detour.

This road was the most harrowing of all. Have you ever driven along a narrow country lane festooned with lemurs' fingers? It is a tricky and ticklish challenge. We laugh in despair while the men who invent these things sit alone in uncarpeted mansions, a dead television in every room, counting and recounting their own senses.

FRINGES AND BANGS

It has started snowing already, which means that snowmen will appear in the gardens of all the houses along my street. This is inevitable, it always occurs when it snows, and years ago I made the assumption that children were responsible for them, just because when I was young the making of snowmen had been one of my favourite occupations in the winter months and I like to think I was good at it too.

My snowmen weren't like men at all. I was more inspired by animals than by people and they would have tusks like a walrus or long necks like giraffes or wide crocodile heads, and a postman once asked me to knock them down because he thought they were quite disturbing. But no, I never did that, I left them standing, and slowly they changed shape, melted and escaped to a place beyond imagination.

In the summer I felt a strong yearning to make snowmen that couldn't be satisfied. My efforts to create snow in the freezer came to nothing. Ice wasn't as much fun. My priorities have changed dramatically and I prefer ovens to fridges now. If I had the space in there, I would keep an oven in my freezer. This illustrates how I have turned my back on the pleasures of the cold. I prefer steam to frosty breath.

There are no children in my street, none at all, and that is why it can't be they who build the snowmen. It took me a long time to work this out. I just wasn't observant enough. Not a single child in any of the houses. My neighbours never touch each other, that's why, and although it is odd that they are legally but not physically married, what right do I have to make a scene about it? I'm the same as they are.

I bake pancakes and they are too hot to eat, so I take them outside on a little shovel and I drape them over the heads of the snowmen that stand in my garden in order to cool them. They look like curious hats, all brim and no crown, on those curious men, and of course there's a secondary motive behind my act. I want to be mischievous, to thaw the misshapen skulls of those pristine figures, these icy intruders.

This is how my winter breakfasts are retributive as well as nourishing, but it's easy for anyone to store up trouble for himself and that's what I'm doing without knowing it. Because it will probably turn out that snowmen are living beings, that these ones are at least, that they venture down from the snowy mountains during blizzards to take up residence in our gardens for purposes unknown, that they are irate.

Have you ever worn a pancake hat? Try it sometime and you will then understand their resentment. I might be forced to sandbag my abode with hot water bottles to keep them out when they resolve to attack together in a special kind of lateral avalanche that resembles a besieging army. I need to prepare for this scenario. I spread maple syrup on my pancakes. I know people who swear by honey. Foul mouths!

I wish I had the ability to weld tubes together to construct a steam gun that would repel invading snowmen through blasts of shrinkage. I require a boiler and coal for that. I can dig for coal in my backyard. I possess big shovels as well as little ones. Has your dwelling ever been surrounded by angry snowmen? It sounds amusing but it is one of those jokes that don't translate well from words into experience.

It is perfectly horrid, in fact. That's why I admire anyone who knocks off a snowman's head in passing with a walking stick. But snowmen are vindictive and will hide their noses in your bags of carrots. And their eyes are made from coal! They flirt with their own destruction. The sights that sear the mind forever? The spark in the snowman's eye is a sign of doom. They are not quite like girls in this respect.

We climb mountains and that's one thing, but sometimes we do so in winter when they are covered in snow and then it is much easier to trick and deceive us. The snow covers everything. This mountain turns out to be a giant hat. That's another way the snowmen get revenge. Verily, they will do everything they can in order to humiliate us. They are flexible as well as frozen, cunning as well as clumsy.

When a beast prowls the neighbourhood at night we can tell what it is by the tracks it leaves. We inspect these with magnifying glasses at dawn or just before lunch. But snowmen leave no tracks when they prowl, only the abominable snowman does that, because he wants to be different. The men of the town claim there is a Bigfoot loose in the forest and we know that the Bigfoot is a near relative of the yeti.

They set off one day with a gigantic sock to capture him. A sock of an unprecedented size, knitted by their unprecedented wives, one so big that it takes thirty men to carry it into the woods. Has anyone ever tried to put a massive sock on Bigfoot before? I think not. I won't expect them back, which is why I didn't go with them, I am more sensible. I drape pancakes on the heads of snowmen. Yes, I'm sensible.

Rain is the enemy of snowmen too. I may do a rain dance at midnight but not on my roof, which isn't flat, because I don't want to slide off and land in the expectant and vicious arms of the snowmen down there. Why is rain supposed to be so fond of dancing? Snowmen pitted by rain are a pitiable sight. In vain they defend themselves with umbrellas but the rain wins in the end. I must fill hot water bottles.

The world is actually a big hot water bottle but full of magma instead of water. The bigger the hot water bottle, the longer it takes to cool. The Earth is so large that it's still hot after billions of years, but one day it will go cold. And the unimaginable cosmic entity it is keeping warm will then have to get out of bed. My head is filled with images of snowmen leaping into the smoking crater of an active volcano.

These idle speculations are useless. I must do something positive that will distract me, exhaust me, calm me down. Otherwise my existence will be like an elbow in mustard, like a reflected grin in soup, a pig in a cloud, a floppy in a brim, a crag in a cloak, and my desires like buckets of jump, rainbow lashes, wonky portfolios, cheese oriels, humdigger handles. Like gusty vents, cogs in mice, grunts in shadow.

I begin to dig for coal in my backyard. That will occupy my hours and erode my worries. Lumps of coal are snowmen eyes. Imagine digging for eyes at this time of the day! I work hard, maybe too hard. I dig deep, then turn to dig sidewise. Weeks pass. Digging for coal, but I only managed to unearth fringes and bangs. Then I realised that I had accidentally tunneled all the way to Germany and it was mine hair.

Monsieur Choux

When he sat on his favourite chair and ate cakes, he was aware that flakes of pastry often stuck to his beard. He would rise ponderously from his comfort and peer at his face in the mirror over the empty fireplace. It was summer and his cat was moulting. He would flick the flakes away with a deft finger and then carefully brush his beard that was rather too long to be fashionable.

The pastry flakes flew into the corners of the

room or went under the table where in the middle of the night a mouse would appear to eat them. The cat would be curled up on the same bed in which the bearded man slept. There was no risk of the mouse being killed and prevented from continuing its work. The flakes would accumulate to an appalling degree without its assistance.

It was a fairly gentle cat anyway and had no hatred for mice. The man was gentle too, apart from when he flicked pastry flakes away, and then he was like an avenging giant. Each time he brushed his beard, a few hairs would come out, pulled from his chin and cheeks by the force of the brush, and these he would scatter over the carpet. He always treated floors as disposal areas.

The cat liked to claw at the carpet and extract individual threads from the weave. At the same time the motion of its paws worked the discarded beard hairs and also its own shed fur into the pattern. This wasn't intentional but it was effective. Over many years, the carpet changed its composition. It began life as a carpet of artificial fibres but was turning into a carpet of hair and fur.

There was more hair than fur in it, to be honest, because the bearded man's face lost more growth in total than did the cat's body. Let's make no bones, he had a large face. Maybe he needed a wife instead of a cat and possibly his beard didn't help him to find one, not that there's anything wrong with beards, but his was just too long and he loved cakes. This has already been said.

His beard also had a little cat fur in it, because the cat liked to rub its head against his chin whenever it had the chance, usually when he was in bed and asleep. And then one day, he realised that the entire carpet was exactly like his beard. It no longer had any artificial fibres left, but was a carpet only of copious beard hair and some fur, a carpet the cat had made over years with its claws.

When a carpet is an analogue of a beard, the things that happen to a beard might also happen to it. This is an ever-present danger. The sky outside the window abruptly darkened and the bearded man got out of his chair to peer out. He saw a colossal man standing in front of the house and this giant's beard was a carpet, mainly of hair with a little cat fur in it, and a flake of pastry too.

The bearded man guessed that this terrible image was only a reflection in a mirror, that the true giant was all around him right now, that his carpet was the real beard. So what was he? A flake of pastry in that beard! Nothing more, nothing less. As the huge fingers came to flick him away, he laughed for the first time in many weeks, but only because he didn't have time to make a speech.

A CORKING TALE

The divers swam slowly but with determination. They were terrified but kept going anyway. This was the greatest distance anyone had ever travelled in a vertical direction. They were pioneers.

They carried the heavy piece of equipment between them. It was awkward and ponderous but they had practised with it for many hours at a safer depth and they were now able to synchronise their movements perfectly. The sharp metal spiral of the tool gleamed faintly.

Both of them were sweating behind their goggles.

Every extra fathom was torment.

They were almost at the limits of their endurance, but they were nearly at their destination. Just a little more effort... Yes! They had reached the base of the curious barrier, its dark underside.

Scientists had already explored the peculiar structure remotely with probes and issued a statement regarding it. Freedom for the entire race lay on the other side, they claimed. This is why two divers had been prepared to risk their lives in order to reach it and pass beyond.

The first diver nodded to the second. They hefted the tool and pushed the tip against the barrier. Then they started turning the handle, trying to make the drill bite. But the metal kept slipping.

They stopped work. One of the divers reached out and touched the barrier, feeling it carefully for several minutes.

"What's the matter?" mutely signalled the other.

The first diver made frantic hand gestures. "It's a screwtop! The scientists got it wrong. It's not a cork after all. It must be cheap plonk. It's not champagne, but cheap Christmas wine! The corkscrew is useless. We're stuck in here forever!"

They began the long swim back to the bottom of the bottle.

DON'T SHOOT THE MESSENGER

A rich man ordered a messenger to deliver an envelope to the king. The messenger set off on the long journey and was never tempted to open the envelope and read the message inside. He assumed it was a Christmas card. The rich man sent many every year.

After weeks of hard travelling, the messenger reached the king, who opened the envelope and read the letter within with a frown that grew deeper and deeper. Finally the king reached for a loaded musket that was by his side and pointed it at the messenger's head.

"Clearly you have received some bad news," said the messenger, "but I'm not responsible for what has happened, so don't shoot the messenger! I completed my given task, that's all."

Silently, but with a grim expression, the king handed the letter to the messenger, who began sweating as he read it. The message said, "Please shoot the messenger who delivers this to you. Merry Xmas."

The king pulled the trigger of the gun and it went off.

All the Waiting

The man is a pedestrian and waiting is a fundamental part of his daily life. He does not drive or ride a bicycle or take giant leaps on spring-loaded legs over rooftops. He walks everywhere and the rain knows his shoulders well. He does not own an umbrella and why should he? The wind that is a typical feature of his city likes to turn them inside out and snatch the fabric canopy off the struts, leaving only a stick sprouting spines. He trudges and waits and crosses the road and the puddles lap over his eroded shoes. Through the holes in these shoes his socks drink the water, quenching their fabric thirst.

If he had the money he would relocate to somewhere warmer, drier, calmer, to a place where waiting is a pleasure and not an imposition. But success is required for money and he has none of that. He is a pedestrian by necessity rather than choice, and for so many years has this been true that he often forgets the fact, forgets that he would exist in a different manner if he could, and when he remembers he stops and frowns, and this pause is an addition to the waiting. He waits for the frown to disperse on his face and then he proceeds to the next kerbside.

The cars hurry past him, metal boxes in which people sit with frowns of their own, velocity grimaces, eyebrows speeding with their attendant faces to some temporary destination. The road is a river of huge bullets that will knock him high or flat with the same result. He must wait. The lights will change, if not this minute then the next, or the next after that, and these minutes slowly accumulate, pile up, add to the pressure of the raindrops on those shoulders of his, hunched a little more every year. The traffic will stop, drivers will scowl as he crosses before them, some will enjoy revving their engines to make him anxious.

Walking in a city is quite a different experience from walking through a rural landscape. The rhythm here is staccato, the ambler must constantly interrupt his flow, his measure, his tempo, because of the numerous and unavoidable streets full of moving traffic that must be crossed. The cars and lorries and motorcycles themselves care not about his cadence, about the pace of a pedestrian, and the drivers and riders and passengers of the vehicles give not the slightest hoot for the dislocations in the joints of the one who must constantly stop moving and start again.

City perambulation is not walking in the purest sense. It is striving, not striding, striving for a harmony that never arrives. Its music is dissonant and atonal. It is a pain in the frame, a jerking of souls in their vessels.

Our pedestrian knows all this and resents the waiting at each kerbside. He wonders how many hours, days, weeks, even months, have amassed in this manner over his lifetime, not only in rain but all kinds of weather, and he dearly wishes that he could obtain a refund, have the waiting given back to him, all of it, every moment, perhaps at the end of his life. And he wishes this so fervently that it becomes a prayer that actually works. The pedestrian dies, an old man at last, worn out by his attritional wanderings through the city, demolished by age, alone in his bedroom one night with the beams from the headlights of passing vehicles moving across the wall, for he has forgotten to close the curtains, and an antique clock ticking on the bedside table, no need to give further details.

And his soul passes to the afterlife, which is an unspecified place, and he finds himself arguing with a nebulous authority there, an administrator of some sort, an officious angel, and he requests repayment of the wasted time, the hours and hours used up in waiting to cross streets and roads, in waiting for cars to take their turn first, as if they are superior to him, those metal, glass and rubber aristocrats that he must submit his human flesh to, and the angel negotiates with him, but he finds himself unable to settle for anything less than every single instant of the time wasted, and remarkably this boon is granted to him. Who knows why?

Perhaps he is so favoured because there is supposed to be some sort of lesson for him in the outcome? He decides to be satisfied with his victory no matter what else transpires. The angel has added up all the time wasted on kerbsides waiting and the final sum stands at exactly four months, two weeks, six days, eighteen hours, twelve minutes and thirty-eight seconds. These will now be returned to the pedestrian. The walls of paradise gleam in the distance of the cloudy plain, but with the tip of a wing the strange angel points away from them. "You must go the other way, my friend, for the world and life are back in that direction."

The pedestrian nods, because this angel has no hands to shake, and he sets off across the featureless landscape and his walking has an unbroken rhythm, the beat he has yearned for, and he is using it to return himself to a second life where he will reclaim the time stolen from him and cheat the traffic that cheated him. His step is joyous. The clouds swirl around him and then they begin to part like shredded drapes and he understands that he is approaching the frontier between the afterlife and the mortal world. He breaks through the final wisps of mist and at last finds himself facing the border and it is not at all what he expected.

It is a road, an immensely wide road, and on the other side is the world but he is stuck on this side and the road is so busy it is fatal to pedestrians and the traffic that speeds down it in both directions is moving so fast that it is a blur, a scream. There is a central reservation but it is so far away he will never reach it. This road has hundreds or even a thousand lanes, each one an awful roar, yet he can see the remote world beckoning to him, the smiles, the spires, the cafés, the flavours and sensations he never properly enjoyed while he was there, and they are all out of reach. With a sigh and a shrug, he resigns himself to waiting at the kerbside until all his refunded time is exhausted. A cross man unable to cross.

THE WRONG LAMP

He bought the thing in a street market and that was a problem because he couldn't take it back and demand the return of his money. The trader had certainly moved on to another location now, for he was the itinerant type and had admitted this at the outset. "I come from far away and tomorrow your city will be the *far away* I come from."

They were curious words spoken in a tone both wistful and defiant. A buyer must beware of such transactions, but the object was something he truly wanted, an example of an outdated futuristic style that both amused him and filled him with nostalgia. He remembered lava lamps when they were fashionable, and now he had one again.

He plugged it in at home but it was a disappointment. Instead of blobs of vibrant colour moving endlessly up and down inside the glass tube and breaking apart and reforming, the lamp merely shone with a dull greenish light and the contents seemed to harden and crystallise. He picked it up to shake it, but no liquid inside moved. Broken?

Perhaps it simply needed to warm up. It was, after all, many years old. The last time lava lamps had adorned the coffee tables of ordinary homes there was fusion jazz on the turntable and trousers widened at the base, a more innocent and garish era. He left it plugged in and went to do chores, then engrossed himself in a book on the sofa.

Once he glanced up and saw that the lamp was changing shape. It was melting and warping, so he disconnected it from the power with a sigh of annoyance, but the green light remained deep within. It must have stored a significant charge inside itself like a battery. He ignored it and returned to his book, the plot of which was fascinating.

The entire narrative seemed to be about to change into something that bore little resemblance to what had transpired so far. This was odd, to say the least, and thrilling. Then he heard a fluttering. His eyes rose out of the page with enormous effort as if extracting themselves from quicksand. He saw the gigantic moth circling the coffee table.

It still contained the green light at the centre of its body and because it is a fact that moths flap around sources of light endlessly, the creature had no choice but to attempt to orbit itself. Then he knew that the trader in the market hadn't cheated him. He had been sold a larva lamp. Such a simple mistake! Aiming carefully, he hurled the book.

THE PANCAKE HURLER

I once reversed the polarity of a dreamcatcher and set the trapped dreams free. That's the kind of man I am. I once released a tray of ice cubes back into the wild by emptying it into the river. Surely when you 'bite the hand that feeds you' you will get more food rather than less? Yes, but I prefer to make and devour pancakes.

To be honest, it's not just about eating them. I like to drape them over things too. In fact I like to hurl them and hope that my aim in conjunction with chance will drape them convincingly over distant targets. I will take a ride on a roller coaster and when I reach the top, I throw pancakes over the side. They fly like edible clocks.

And yes, sometimes they land on people down below, and I have seen more than one bald man wearing one of my pancakes on his head. But the oddest occasion was when one landed on the apex of a tall pointy hat that a woman was wearing. It was stuck there and span round and round like a vinyl record. Remember those?

Have you ever looked at a map of Antarctica and thought it resembled a pancake? I have and still do. It looks like a pancake that is stuck on the protruding South Pole, the same way that a pancake might get stuck on a pointy hat, but I don't really believe that anyone hurled it on. It must have got there by some other method.

But how? I was baffled for a long time by this question. Then one day I was peering through a microscope at an amoeba in a drop of water and I saw at once that this amoeba wasn't like others of its kind. It had a desire to explore, to venture beyond its surroundings and maybe discover other water drops previously unknown to it.

It possessed what has come to be known as the 'explorer gene' and it would never be satisfied to remain within its own bubble of reality. As I watched, it pushed out of its confinement and began wandering in search of new worlds. It eventually found one, on the opposite cheek, a drop of liquid identical to the one it had left.

Because these drops were actually tears on the face of a scientist who was shedding them, and she was shedding them because of her failure to prove the explorer gene existed or didn't exist, I can't recall which. How ironic is this? Very, is the answer! Sorry Dolores! I know you regard my attentions as intrusive. I will take the microscope away.

Antarctica is not a giant pancake, after all. It is a colossal amoeba and all the other continents are amoebas too. Plate tectonics have nothing to do with the way they wander across the globe. They move because amoebas move and Antarctica went further because it was the most curious, but it got stuck on the pole and can't free itself.

The geographical poles really are lengths of metal that stick up. In fact they are the ends of one vast rod that passes right through the planet. But ice covers them, which is why we have never yet seen them and why you don't believe in them now. I will make pancakes before Dolores comes home and I will hurl all of them at her.

The majority will miss and some will sail through open windows and land on cats, and others will soar into the next room and drape themselves over the robot who dwells there, and one might even spin out of this story and end up on your face, covering it like a mask and preventing you from reading any words that come after this one.

The Precious Mundanity

After the boy was tucked up snugly in bed, the mother kissed his forehead but she didn't turn to leave. Then the boy said, "I'm so excited about tomorrow I don't think I'll ever get to sleep!"

She smiled at him and patted the sheets, but her face was sad. "There's something I need to tell you," she said.

His eyes widened in response. "You don't mean I'm not adopted?"

"Don't be silly." She laughed. "Why would I lie about that? You've always known my husband isn't your real father. No, it's something else. You're seven years old now and it's time you learned the truth."

"I don't understand, mother," he answered.

She sighed and regarded the simple bedroom. They were a poor family and lived in a very modest house in a shabby town. Outside, the sun had already set, but the sky still held enough light to illuminate the people trudging up the dusty street. A donkey began braying and kicking a clay wall; elsewhere the tradesmen and merchants were shutting their shops. A pale moon rose over the low hills. A normal evening.

"It's about Christmas," she said.

He was sitting up in bed now, blinking at her. "Yes?"

"Father Christmas in particular…"

His eyes lit up at the mention of this name. "Last year he brought me a toy boat and the year before that he gave me a ball and the year before that…" He caught his breath and added, "I can't wait to see what he'll give me tomorrow!"

She placed a finger over his lips and shook her head. "That's exactly what I must tell you. Father Christmas doesn't actually exist. It's your father who brings you those gifts. Your real father. That's the truth."

"What?" He was distraught. "You mean there's no such thing as Santa Claus? The jolly fat man in red with a sack over his shoulder is just a myth? A lie?"

"I'm afraid so. Your father pretends to be him."

"My father? My real father? The supernatural force that created the universe? The omniscient, omnipotent lord of everything? Oh mother! You've turned Christmas into a magical occasion. You've destroyed the mundanity of it! The precious mundanity! I'll never forgive you for this. Never!"

"My poor son," She reached out to hug him close to her, but he pounded his little fists against her and then fell back on the bed and turned on his side. She spoke to his bristling back. "I'm sorry to break the news this way. Santa Claus is from the future, you see. That's why your father keeps up the pretence. Even Christmas hasn't been invented yet!"

But it was no use. He wasn't listening. She rose and quietly left Jesus sobbing into his pillow.

The most unbearable night of the year passes with excruciating slowness. And yet it passes. The sun rises in the east, as it always does, and we wake up and open our eyes and we are alive, as we usually are.

AND
NOW IT
IS XMAS DAY!

THE SHOCKING STOCKING

Christmas has come once again and as always the stocking is waiting at the foot of the bed. It is bulging full. What can be inside it? The child is excited and can't wait to find out. Throwing off the bedclothes, he leaps out and scurries on little bare feet to investigate. Will it contain toys and sweets, nuts and chocolates? It has never been this full before. He thrusts his hand into the opening and pulls out…

A severed leg. What a strange present to receive! The child is baffled. What use is such a horrid leg to him? He already has two of his own and they are perfectly fine. This one is dry and leathery and obviously old. It probably was amputated decades ago. Disappointed, the child examines it with a sullen expression. He lifts it up to shake it. The leg is hollow and many things are rattling inside, but what?

He peers into the stump of the thigh. It is like looking into some weird sort of kaleidoscope. There are shifting lights, moving scenes, voices too, as if the leg contains communities of tiny people. Then he understands. It is full of stories, this leg, stories suitable for the season. But what types of stories exactly? True or made up? The answer is obvious. Leg ends. That is what they are. Strange modern legends.

TARZAN IN INDIA

This is a little known incident in the life of the famous lord of the jungle. He was passing near a lake in a volcano crater when the fumes overcame him. It was still an active volcano and the heat inside sometimes bubbled fumes through the water that came out to drift through the foliage and incapacitate anyone who happened to be near. Tarzan collapsed and lay unmoving on the floor of the dense jungle.

He was found the following day by a band of slavers who happened to be in the region. The volcano had settled down now and no fumes were percolating through the lake. The slavers picked him up and carried him to the nearest port and sold him to the captain of a ship bound for India. Still unconscious, Tarzan only awoke when the ship began breaking up in a wild storm off the coast of Goa. Everyone else was drowned. He swam through the waves and reached the shore.

He had no idea where he was, but he picked himself up and began his wanderings. He met an old man with a matted beard and long fingernails and they engaged in a brief conversation. The man told Tarzan about the gods and goddesses and how they should best be worshipped with acts of extreme asceticism. But the lord of the jungle soon grew perturbed and doubtful. "Me Tarzan, you Hindu," he said.

He walked on and met another old man but this one had a shaved head and wore a saffron robe and carried a begging bowl. He told Tarzan that the answer to life was to cast off worldly attachments, to find the middle way, to remain aloof to both the pleasures and pains of the world, to seek serenity in meditation and chanting. But the lord of the jungle yawned deeply. "Me Tarzan, you Buddhist," he said.

As he wandered onwards, he finally met a third man. This man wore simple garments and swept the ground carefully before him to reduce the chances of treading on insects, and wore a mask over his nose and mouth to avoid breathing them in. He told Tarzan that the best holy life involved causing as little suffering to all living things as possible, plants included. Tarzan felt something stir inside him and he knew that this was the right path for him. "Me Tarzan, you Jain," he said.

NOOKIE NOCKING

A man guessed his wife was having an affair so he followed her with a bow and arrow. In the woods he saw her cuddling her lover, so he nocked an arrow and let it fly. It thudded into a nearby tree but the illicit lovers were so engrossed in each other they didn't even notice.

 The man went home. Later his wife returned. "Missed me, darling?" she asked in a cheery voice. "Yes!" growled the man.

THE COCKNEY KHARMS

Comfy in that doorway, are you? Waiting for a man, is it? As long as it's not a cockney geezer, strike a light me ol' china guvnor, I think you'll be fine, just fine, you'll be, wait and see. I gives friendly advice like this when I'm out and about, I does. Thank you too. You're gone and been a right old upright pint of milk stout by saying that, bless your knees up! Me heart is touched, it is.

 Dodgy men everywhere in this part of the city. Met one only the other day, I did, in broad daylight, no less. That's bleeding right, that is, barrows and carts, did 'im in with an eel pie, I did, well what he said to me was a blooming cheek, it was, right in me face when I was crossing the threshold out of The Slippery Git, so I slapped 'is cheeks with the pie, is what I did. Stale and all.

He ain't said nuffink to me since, well how could he what with that swollen mug of his, and a mug without a handle neither! What 'e said to me don't bear repeating, it don't, burned me ears right off, fell on that floor they did, crisp and charred, and a dog ran up and ate the bleeders. He didn't so much run as hop, only had one 'orrid hairy leg, the poor ugly monstrosity, been around the pubs he has.

So what you going to do if he don't turn up, your man? You willing to accept an alternative man, someone like me, I can show you the sights, take you down to the river, row you out on a giant floating eel pie, we bloody use eel pies for everyfing in this flipping place, and ride the currents past the old gallows where the butchers hung bloody aprons up to dry in the bit nippy winds.

Oh, pardon me, I didn't see the gash right across your throat, all the bleeding way around. Been murdered already, has you? What man are you waiting for then? I see, the undertaker, is it, that makes sense. Pardon me for interrupting, I'll just be on my way, with a merry little tune in the whistle of my lips. I can do that because I'm just a cheeky cockney chappie, what nuffink do dismay.

Why are you throwing me under the wheels of this passing omnibus? Was being friendly, I was, no more than that. What's the bleeding world coming to? Now I am dead too, flat as an eel without 'is pie, and what's keeping the blooming undertaker, I ask you, drunk as usual, I bet, him and his missus always at the formaldehyde, pair of scoundrels, gagging on that liquid, the blighters!

"What is a Kharms?" wonders the child and he is surprised and alarmed by a voice that replies from somewhere inside the empty stocking. "Don't worry too much about that," it whispers, "because you will find out soon enough if you keep viewing the tales."

The child doesn't lower the leg or remove his eye from it. He supposes that the voice belongs to the original owner of the limb, that once upon a time it was part of a whole person. The voice has become detached and is living an independent existence at last, but this doesn't concern the child too much. The leg belongs to him now.

THE LOG

I had difficulties sleeping, so I went to a doctor and said, "I want to sleep like a log," and he raised his eyebrows and said:

"Are you sure?"

"Yes, I am. Absolutely."

He gave me medicine and that same night I drank it, but my sleep was even worse than before. Be careful what you ask for, that's what they say, and now I believe them. I'll never go back to that doctor.

I slept like a log last night... Full of bitter nostalgia for the tree I once had been and terrified of being thrown on a fire!

Wrexham Chainsaw Massacre

In the dark they huddled and utterly silent they were. Beyond the walls lay Wrexham, an unprepossessing town that literally throbbed in the endless Welsh rain.

The adults held their children tightly, ready to stifle any whine or scream. Silence was essential for continued life. They listened for the growl that would announce horror and destruction.

At last it came, a powerful rumble from far away, growing louder as it moved closer to this place of inadequate safety. The youngsters started to panic and in the thick darkness their terror was contagious. Everyone began talking loudly.

"Shh! You'll give our location away!"

"Don't be stupid. He already knows we're here. He has been planning this for a long time. We can't hide anymore and we can't run. There's no escape at all!"

"I'm not giving up without a fight..."

"Nor me. I may be a bit rusty, but is that any reason to condemn me to death in such a brutal manner?"

"When he breaks in, we must attack him together."

"Yes, that's our only hope!"

"Get ready everyone! Any second now..."

The rumbling grew even louder. An unseen force flung the warehouse doors open. And there he was. Twenty metric tonnes of implacable steamroller, trundling forward without mercy, crushing all who stood in his path. The chainsaws started themselves up and cut pointlessly at the solid metal cylinder of his roller. But even if they had been healthy power tools in their prime, such desperate resistance would have been futile.

The entire collection of redundant stock was relentlessly ground into atoms by the cruel colossus.

Oil spurted up the walls and made stagnant pools in the corners. Dust settled.

The Wrexham chainsaw massacre was over.

"Wrexham is a town in Wales," explains the voice from the stocking and the child snorts and says, "Does it really matter where it is? I don't plan to ever go there. If you must speak to me about locations only do so if it's relevant to the outcome of the story."

The voice ignored him and said, "The question is why the chainsaws were given the gift of consciousness in the first place? They never wanted to be sentient. It was probably the fault of a mad inventor who specialises in such things. An inventor with almost limitless funds and no bothersome regulations to stifle his odd and unethical imagination, the sort of genius who designs deadly fairground rides."

THE OPPOSITE OF MOONS

It occurred to me while I was having a haircut this morning that full moons make people more hairy by turning them into werewolves, and barbers make people less hairy by cutting their hair.

So barbers are the opposite of moons.

What is the opposite of the moon? The sun!

So barbers are suns. But sons of whom?

Of their fathers, of course! And 'father' sounds like 'farther'. What is farther than many other things?

Farther than all barber shops, for example?

The moon! Therefore barbers are the sun and the moon at the same time. They make people less hairy, by cutting their hair, and also more hairy, by turning them into werewolves.

This makes good business sense.

FATE AND THE WARRIOR

Fate whispers to the warrior, "You cannot withstand the storm." And the warrior whispers back, "I am the storm."

"Yes, you are a bit of a windbag," agrees Fate. To which the warrior replies, "Oh, that's a bit nasty, isn't it?"

And Fate says, "Speak up, I can't hear you in this roaring gale, you pompous pluvial barometric buffoon."

RASPBERRIES

I had a yen for raspberries.

Then I remembered that 'yen' is not only a yearning but also the unit of currency in Japan.

At current exchange rates, one yen is worth £0.0066.

The cheapest going rate for raspberries in Britain at this moment in time is £1.29 for 150 grams.

The average weight of an individual raspberry is 4 grams. Therefore the price of one raspberry is £0.344.

This means that with one yen I am able to afford 1/52nd of a single raspberry. In other words, a mere 2% of one fruit.

The lesson from all this?

Be very careful what you have a yen for!

The Race

Bossy Boots versus Clever Clogs.

Who would win in a race?

Neither type of footwear is suitable for athletic competitions, but I always assumed that boots would have the advantage of staying on while clogs would fly off into the crowd.

Then I thought about it more carefully.

The boots and clogs are racing on their own, without feet inside them, so there is nothing for the clogs to fly off *from*.

They are clogs that move by some mysterious motive power, the same power that enables the boots to take part in this sporting event.

Also the clogs are clever.

They might have a clever way of evading all potential disasters during the dash.

But the boots are bossy.

It is conceivable they may order the clogs to lose the race. Will the clogs take heed?

Maybe they will. Clogs are daft, so daft that even clever clogs are not that bright. They might do as they are told without question.

And talking about questions, I have always wondered about clogs. About the hazards they must be daily subjected to.

Splinters, flammability, whether if they step in a puddle they will float away like a pair of boats, squirrels, illegal loggers. I don't trust them. But as for boots, are they any better?

Hardly! Boots trampled all over the countries of our bruised continent not so many years ago. The rhythm of the marching was like the pulse of a violent heart, the heart of a giant.

And this giant, who was so huge and mean and domineering, lived inside the frame of a small man, because he was a giant in metaphorical terms only.

The giant still lives inside that man, yes he does.

And this man has a name you know.

And now I will ask two different questions that miraculously have the same answer…

Can Napoleon conquer most of Europe?

And what's his nationality?

Course he can!

"Course he can what?" wonders the child, and the voice says, "Citizen, of course." To which the irritated child responds indignantly, "Course he can citizen! That makes no sense to me."

And the voice is impatient as it answers, "That's because you are still a child and not an adult and also have never been to the island."

"Why would I want to go there?"

"It belongs to France, just as Paris does, and France is full of famous writers. A famous French writer once stole some roasting corn-on-the-cobs off my beach barbecue, and I never saw his face but I knew, just knew, that he was Robbe-Grillet."

THE MISCREANT

Whenever he climbed the luxuriously carpeted stairs to my room in bare feet he always groaned with pleasure, and that's how I knew, just knew, that Cocteau was coming.

BLOCKING THE FLUE

The tour of the cracker factory ended in disaster. It should have been obvious from the beginning it was a bad idea. The building exploded and the brick walls fell into the lake, creating a tsunami that engulfed a dozen fishermen and almost as many boats. Ever since, this terrible incident has been known as: Cracker Tour.

The witch had broken her broomstick. It was still under warranty, so she contacted the manufacturer and asked for a replacement. They sent her a balloon instead, but the canopy was missing. "How can I fly in just a basket?" she cried. The representative who had delivered it told her not to worry because it was a: Wicca Basket.

The levitating basket stalled after an hour, plummeting with its occupant down the main chimney of a cracker factory, blocking the flue. There was a build up of gas. Hence the explosion. An investigation is pending. And a concluding pun is on its way.

THE HIDEOUS CACKLE

"Come in to my spider," said the pantry to the ghost.

The ghost tugged at its chin in deep consternation. It knew there was something wrong in what had just been said to it; not just the fact that it is impossible for an inanimate object such as a pantry to talk, but something in the actual *substance* of what was said didn't ring true, in the same way a bell made of human bones might not.

"I'm not sure I want to," answered the ghost mildly.

"Oh, but you must!" cried the pantry with a hideous cackle. "Because my spider is very keen to meet you."

"Is he really?" The ghost was even more concerned.

"Yes, he's *dying* to meet you!"

"D-d-d-d-d-dying!" gasped the ghost in horror.

"Ha ha ha!" shrieked the pantry as it opened its door of a mouth. And the ghost knew that the pantry was a psychopath and that it had to float, float, float away, as fast as its ectoplasm could take it! And the cackles of that hideous cackling followed him.

"Let me out! Let me out of this haunted house!"

"It's not a house," chided a mysterious voice, "but a cottage, a spooky cottage, and you will never ever leave."

"W-w-w-w-who are you?" gasped the poor ghost.

"I am the lounge!" chuckled the lounge.

The ghost knew that every room in the building was in league against it, but there was nothing it could do to save itself. And a bleak chill mist descended over the cottage and everything became grey and existentialist and bleak and critically acclaimed in certain small but vigorous corners of the literary scene and so that was that…

Fossilised Hurricanes

Circular houses can survive hurricanes when ordinary shaped houses are smashed to splinters. This is because they resemble fossilised hurricanes, those houses. The real hurricanes will take a detour around them because they think such houses are their ancestors.

I saw a film about this once.

Not a documentary but a feature film.

My favourite films are only those that other people have never heard of, such as *Après Couscous de Baguette* directed by Alphonse Doodah, which I just invented and which won the palme d'face one year, I can't remember which. The performance of Isabelle Lovely was great. I loved the way her pouting lips were in black and white while everything else in the film was in colour. There was a hurricane in this film too but only at night, so it never appeared on screen.

Cheaper that way, I guess. But Alphonse Doodah did direct a film in a storm only last year. No artificial illumination was used, only the flashes of sheet lightning. Isabelle Lovely was electrocuted but her monochrome lips survived and will appear in his next film, at least according to people I know in the business, the lip service.

Sheet lightning is when the notes of the associated thunder have been precisely composed beforehand. It is the opposite of improvised or jazz lightning. And now I need a coffee…

"I am feeling agitated now," says the child, "because I am unsure what I am supposed to be learning from these stories. They aren't scary and yet my heart rate has increased noticeably."

"Calm yourself," the disembodied voice urges.

"Ah, you are talking about Kharms again! You promised that I would soon understand the meaning of it."

"Daniil Kharms was a man, a writer born in 1905 in St Petersburg in the country of Russia. After criticism from the Soviet authorities his books were suppressed and he found himself unable to publish

anything, yet he continued writing. He specialised in absurd and rather monstrous flash fictions that often featured people falling out of windows. Imprisoned, he was deliberately starved to death."
"That's not very nice."
"The following two tales are in his style."

KHARMS BEFORE THE STORM

Kharms said to Lakoba, "Do you mind if I ask you a question?"
Lakoba answered, "No, go ahead."
Kharms remained silent.
Lakoba gasped, "Well? Go on, I'm waiting!"
Kharms frowned. "Waiting for what?"
Lakoba cried, "For the question!"
Kharms replied, "But I asked it and you gave me your answer. I asked, do you mind if I ask you a question? That was my question. And you answered: no, go ahead."
Lakoba reddened. "In that case you asked your question before I gave you my permission to ask it."
Kharms said, "Does that make you angry?"
Lakoba bellowed, "Livid!"
Kharms shrugged. "Nonetheless I am satisfied."
Without hesitation, Lakoba rushed at Kharms, twisted his arms behind his back and threw him out the window.

KEEP KHARMS AND BE AN ABSURDIST

Ivan Oknov was a man with red hair and one black tooth. He bumped into another man on the corner of

Askance Street. The other man had black hair and one red tooth and his name was Navi Vonko.

"You bumped into me," Navi said.

"No, you bumped into me," responded Ivan.

"I think it was you into me."

"On the contrary, it was you into me."

"But I was already bumped into, by you, when I bumped into you," Navi argued and his tone was so fierce that it became entirely reasonable to believe his version of events. So Ivan said:

"Very well, have it your way. But what's the rush anyway?"

"I'm rushing to work, that's where," said Navi.

"Me too," said Ivan. "To work."

"I make money doing what I love to do," declared Navi.

"What might that be?" asked Ivan.

"Advising people on how to make money doing what they love to do," came the reply. "That's what I love to do and I get paid for doing it. I get paid in money, real money, for that. What do you do?"

"I do what I don't love doing. I wring the necks of clocks."

"Wring the necks of clocks," you said?

"I said that, exactly that."

"Well, I can show you how to make money doing what you love to do instead. I can show you in ten minutes."

"I wouldn't like that," said Ivan uneasily.

"Why not? Why not?" Navi cried.

"Because I love to lose money, that's what I love to do; and if I made money doing that, if I made money losing it, then I would never lose any, and I wouldn't be doing what I love doing, which is losing money, so how could I make money doing what I love? It's impossible."

Navi considered this carefully. A truck was approaching down the road. Suddenly he grabbed hold of Ivan and threw himself into the path of the vehicle and they were both crushed to death.

"I think that Russia must be a frightening place," says the child, and then he asks the voice, "Are you from there?"

"Absolutely not. I am from a place beyond your imagination, from an abyss of nightmares, from a chasm of catastrophe, a gorge of gore, from a place so remote that it stretches right around the universe and back and is lurking next to you at this very moment, from a cavern filled with dead shrieking souls, from a pit of pendulums."

"Why are you here now?"

"Because I was destined to come."

KNOCK! KNOCK!

The author Richard Hughes wrote, "When destiny knocks the first nail in the coffin of a tyrant, it is seldom long before she knocks the last."

In fact this is the opening line of chapter five of his famous novel *A High Wind in Jamaica* and it seems to be awfully true.

"Knock! Knock!"

"Who's there?"

"The first nail in the coffin of a tyrant."

"The first nail in the coffin of a tyrant who?"

"The first nail in the coffin of a tyrant who wants you to know that the second knock in the 'knock knock' above is the last nail in the coffin of a tyrant and that you are the tyrant."

SUN SOUP

This is my recipe for sun soup. First take a sunflower, and then carefully cut away the flower, leaving the sun. Put the sun in a cauldron and add a deep ocean. Garnish with moonstones and it's ready! The best thing about sun soup is that it goes down beautifully.

NOT A REAL POEM

I wrote a faux five-word poem. It goes like this:
See Esther / take a / siesta
And then I thought about turning it into a faux eight-word poem by adding the words: *in the nude*.
But I didn't, because that's rude.

IN MY OWN HANDS

I took my life into my own hands.
But my life was contained in my entire body, so I took my entire body into my own hands.
My own hands are part of my entire body.
So I took my own hands into my own hands.
But my own hands were already holding my entire body, including my own hands, which were holding my entire body, including my own hands, which were

holding my entire body, including my own hands, and so on forever, so there simply wasn't any room.
    Damn those figures of speech!

The Figure of Speech

She had a great figure of speech.
    I metaphor a drink and tried to coax a simile.
    She said, "I never cheat when I play on words."
    I went home alone…

"These tales are very short," complains the child, "in fact they are too short and I feel somewhat cheated."
    "Well, you are short too," points out the voice.
    "But that's because I am still growing. One day I will be big but the tales in this leg will never change."
    "How do you know you are still growing? Look at me, for example. I am older than you but I am just a voice and a voice on its own isn't taller than any other object in the world. But don't be dismissive of short tales. The author Brian Aldiss invented a subgenre called the 'Mini-Saga'. The idea is to write a short story with a beginning, middle and end in exactly 50 words. The title is not included in the word count but shouldn't exceed fifteen words. Some mini-sagas can be very entertaining. The next pair of stories are mini-sagas. Pay attention!"

A Post-Disaster Story

Scientists had no way of stopping the asteroid. A postal worker had an idea. He went into space in a rocket and fixed a stamp to it. Now it was the responsibility of the Post Office. They typically failed to deliver it correctly. It struck Mars. The Earth was saved.

Pretty Face

He would do anything for a pretty face. When his wife caught him stealing her makeup there was a struggle. She fell and hit her head on the bedside cabinet. He went to fetch the scissors. And now he wears her face over his own and it is pretty. Awful.

"That's all very well," says the child, "but I'm in the mood for something longer now, or I may become bored."

"Very well," concedes the voice. "I am sure there must be one or two longer pieces somewhere in the depths of the leg, perhaps near the ankle or inside the feet themselves. But I suspect they will be followed by more very short pieces before the leg runs out."

"The leg will run out? But it's not connected to a body."

"Run out of tales, I mean…"

The Unfair Funfair

"But that's unfair!" protested Benjamin.

"Life is unfair," said Karl.

"This isn't life, it's the weekend, and I have every right to come with you to the fairground today."

"You have no rights at all. You are a boy."

"But you promised!"

Karl sighed and considered the matter. His son was glaring up at him with all the solicitous viciousness of a juvenile weasel that was ready to pounce and rip out his throat, not that Karl had ever seen that happen or even imagined it until this moment.

"Do you understand what kind of fairground it is?"

Benjamin pouted. "No."

Karl said, "It's not like the ones you have been to before. This one is a new kind of thing, with 'thing' being the important word in that sentence. It's a small but insane place. Frabjal Troose designed it. He is completely mad and very rich. The roller coasters are said to be cruelly fatal and I've heard that the Ghost Train has real werewolves inside. I am not planning to actually go on any of the rides."

"What's the point then?" wondered Benjamin.

"I want to watch others die."

"But that's horrid. Why do you want that?"

"Because they betrayed me."

"All of them betrayed you, father? But how?"

"It's complicated," said Karl.

He bit his lip and turned away. How could be explain to his son what a misanthrope was? The boy was too young for such a long word. All his ideas were still in the process of developing. And his ego was also far too small at this stage to make him a useful ally, one who would understand. If you put your ego on the line, don't be surprised when the line turns out to be a noose! Karl said gruffly:

"I'll bring you back some heads, if you like."

"Why would I want heads?"

"With full heads of hair, son! Not bald heads."

"I still don't understand…"

"Three blond heads and one dark head."

"Only one dark head?"
"Yes, few people with black hair go on the rides."
"But just one dark head is—"
"Yes, son, you are quite right. It's not fair."

Forgetting Faces

I never forget a face but that's because I don't remember them in the first place, so there is nothing to forget. The reason I don't remember them is that I don't possess a brain. I am not a man or a robot. I am a black stone, a rock that fell from space millennia ago.

Some people come from very far away to the remote location where I sit in my comfortable crater and they examine me carefully. At first these people were pilgrims, then they tended to be scientists. They are surprised by how black I am, my lustrous darkness.

They describe my colour as "so black it is almost blue" and this really is bewildering for me. Surely there is nothing so black as black? How can blue be blacker? It is equivalent to saying, "This woman's behaviour is so typical of Jane that she must be Amanda."

It makes no sense, no sense at all. I sit in my crater and flex my facets in the sun and then flex them back again at night as they cool. I am happy here and my happiness partly stems from the fact I have no memory. The scientists who prod me are soon forgotten.

And now I see you peering at your own reflection in my surface. I am so black I am almost blue. That's what you are about to say. But who are you? Let me meet your gaze. I never forget a face for the reasons outlined above. You are opening your medical bag.

You rummage inside and remove a stethoscope, with which you listen to my heart, deep within my mass. All your movements are so typical of a certain doctor I know that it's clear you must be someone else. So black it is blue and so precise it is quite a shambles.

METAFICTION

Metafiction.
    Married a fiction.
    Had lots of little microfictions
    just like this one.
    I'm a fiction too. A parable
    in which nothing goes right.
    Why, O why, is God
    publishing me?

GERONIMO

The college girls were baring their behinds out of the dormitory window on the night my parachute jump went wrong.

And they say the moon landings were faked?

X MARKS THE SPOT

"Please come back to me," pleaded the man.

The woman merely wrote on a clipboard with a red pen. "I give the pimple on your nose six out of ten," she said.

Life After Death

This is my thinking on the subject of life after death. When I am dead I will be dead, but while I am dead there will be other people who are born who call themselves "me" and that's exactly the same thing as me calling myself "me" now, because to them they will be me, just as I am me to me now. This applies equally to everyone.

In other words, there will be life after death because after your death others will be alive. This isn't the same thing as reincarnation because there will be no survival of your identity. It just means that someone else will be locked inside a random head and will say "I" and "me" just as you do now, and you might as well be that person, the same way you already came from nothing and became you.

Does this make sense?

The child lowers the leg from his eye. It has stopped working. There are no more legends in this leg end. Is it broken? He shakes it and it rattles but the stories have stopped. Maybe there were only 28 in total. This doesn't really matter. His main presents are waiting for him under the tree in the living room. He throws the leg into a corner and jumps off the bed. But he has a dreadful surprise…

One of his own legs is missing, the left one! It must have disappeared while he was engrossed in the stories. He is annoyed. He will have to hop all the way down the stairs now. His parents will be angry with him. How could he be so unfortunate as to lose a limb like this? Tears roll down his face and his lower lip trembles. Where can it be now? Will it return of its own accord or has it vanished forever?

And somewhere far away, a smaller child draws out a smaller severed leg from a smaller stocking and frowns.

Printed in Great Britain
by Amazon